THE POWERS
HAVEN'S LEGACY

BOOK TWO

MELISSA BENOIST & JESSICA BENOIST

Cataloging-in-Publication Data has been applied for and may be obtained from the Library of Congress.

ISBN 978–1-4197–5263–6

Jacket illustrations by Erwin Madrid
Text © 2023 Melissa Benoist and Jessica Benoist-Young
Book design by Deena Micah Fleming

Printed and bound in U.S.A.

10 9 8 7 6 5 4 3 2 1

Amulet Books are available at special discounts when purchased in quantity for premiums and promotions as well as fundraising or educational use. Special editions can also be created to specification. For details, contact specialsales@abramsbooks.com or the address below.

Amulet Books® is a registered trademark of Harry N. Abrams, Inc.

ABRAMS The Art of Books
195 Broadway, New York, NY 10007
abramsbooks.com

For our mother, who immersed us in the endless ocean of possibilities that are a love of reading and a good personal library

CHAPTER ONE

The compass needle quivered slightly but kept its aim. There was no mistaking its target—the woman in the doorway.

Ellie blinked, looking down at the compass and back up again. It was almost too much to believe. Standing at the threshold was her mom's twin sister, Sadie. Ellie and Parker's aunt.

Before this summer, the twins hadn't even known Sadie existed—their late mother had never once mentioned her. And they certainly hadn't expected to see her so soon after the fiasco that had just gone down at Haven. Yet here she was, the woman with the very same face Ellie most longed to see— but belonging to the wrong person.

Their father stood in the vestibule, blocking Sadie from entering the house. It was beyond weird to see someone who looked so much like their mom standing right next to him, and in their own home, no less. Ellie could feel her insides tying themselves in knots.

"It's late and I—I don't understand what this is about," their father stammered. "What do you want? I mean, can I help you?"

Ellie's eyes scanned Aunt Sadie again, then looked over at Parker. Her sister seemed equally stunned, mouth agape, cheeks flushed. Ellie wasn't sure if her eyebrows could possibly climb any higher up her forehead.

What do we say? Ellie absorbed Parker's thoughts, tinged with her sister's typical hundred-mile-per-hour urgency. *Why is she here? What does she want? Do you think we can trust her?*

Ellie didn't have an answer for any of it.

Parker glanced down at the compass quivering in Ellie's hand. *If the compass pointed at her, maybe she's trustworthy?*

"I hope so." Ellie settled on the step to watch the action unfold.

It was curious that the compass tugged in Sadie's direction, as it seemed to have a knack for pointing toward good things, like leading the twins to safety, or directing them toward their fate. By now Ellie knew it was no accident—like the other objects their mom had left for them, the compass was meant to tell them something. They just needed to figure out what that something was.

Sadie fixed her sparkling gaze on their father. "I'm so sorry to show up unannounced, and at bedtime, no less," she said. "With everything you've been through lately, I know you don't need another surprise. But I didn't have any other choice. I promise you, it's very, very important."

"Important as in urgent?" their dad raked a hand through his hair, the way he did whenever he got caught in traffic or when the Internet cut out for no apparent reason. "Is someone in danger? Are *we* in danger? Can this possibly wait until morning?"

What's he so shaken up about? Arlo's voice hummed in her head as he slipped up the stairs and settled on the step below the girls. *It's just that Sadie lady. It's not like the Danger is here.* He sighed and daintily crossed his front paws, resting his scruffy chin on top. Ellie loved when he crossed his paws that way. It always looked like he was about to have his portrait taken.

"Nothing needs to be done tonight, but I do think it's best that we talk now." Sadie's calm, soothing manner felt comforting and familiar. It reminded Ellie of their mother.

She doesn't seem like a killer, Parker thought.

"Yeah, but neither did Mabel," Ellie hissed under her breath.

Aunt Mabel's words echoed through Ellie's mind. *Sadie killed your mom.* Was it true? Had Sadie come to confess? Even though nothing Mabel said or did was trustworthy, Ellie thought it wise to be cautious around Sadie. If there was anything this strange summer had taught her, it was to trust no one. (Except her own twin.) If only there was some test they could perform, some way to tell if Sadie was best avoided.

Then it hit her. "Wait. The whistle!"

Jumping up, she scrambled back to her room and began rummaging through the bag she had yet to unpack from Haven. Somewhere in there was another gift from her mother, a whistle that was seemingly only audible to those with bad intentions. She rooted around until she felt the cool metal of the tiny instrument, yanked it out of the depths of her duffel as if pulling a clam from mud, then quickly rejoined Parker at the top of the staircase.

Good idea! Parker thought at Ellie.

"Thanks," Ellie whispered. Arlo's eyes glinted in approval.

Below them, Dad and Sadie were engaged in hushed conversation as Ellie took a deep breath and blew the whistle as hard as she could. Her cheeks puffed up like a blowfish while Parker whipped around to gauge Sadie's reaction. Ellie gave the whistle another round of staccato blows for good measure.

Sadie prattled on, oblivious. The whistle didn't faze her one bit; her warm smile hadn't even faltered.

Well, that's a relief, Parker thought to Ellie. Maybe the whistle wasn't the *official* way to tell if Sadie could be trusted, but Ellie hoped it was a sign that she wasn't an *immediate* threat.

"Wait, what did you just say?" Their dad's voice suddenly rose several octaves, cutting through the soft hum of Sadie's mutters and Arlo's rustling exhales.

Both girls snapped to attention.

"She's alive," Sadie told him gently, dropping any lingering pretense of discretion. "Ginny is alive."

Parker jolted so violently that she ended up one step below where she'd started. Arlo pulled himself to standing, then stretched, flexing his toes. Ellie stilled. Ginny—their mom—alive?

"That's why I'm here," Sadie finished, tucking a strand of her long black hair behind her ear.

Ellie's dad drew a breath. "I don't know what to say." He paused for what felt like the longest minute Ellie had ever experienced, then shook his head violently. "How dare you. Is this some kind of sick joke?"

"No!" Parker interjected, before Sadie could respond. "Wait!" She was down the stairs in a flash.

Ellie's heart, she realized, sounded not dissimilar to her sister's tromping footfalls. *Thud-thud-thud-thud-THUD.*

"Parker—" Their dad held his hand up like a crossing guard trying to stop Parker's advance, but Ellie knew no earthly force could possibly keep her sister from bombarding Sadie with questions.

"Where is she?" Parker demanded.

"Well—"

Parker barely left Sadie a chance to eke out one word before she barreled on to the next question.

"Is she *here*?!" Parker asked, her volume rising. "Is she okay? Is she close? Can we see her?"

Ellie's stomach fluttered as she descended the stairs to join the others. Arlo nudged her hand and looked up at her with his big brown eyes.

I know, it's a shock, but good news on the whole, he reminded her. *Maybe the best news.* His dog voice was reassuring against the other thoughts swirling inside her head.

Ellie nodded, but she could feel the corners of her lips tugging downward. If their mom was alive as Sadie claimed, where was she? Why had she chosen to stay away for so long? Didn't she want to be with them?

"No, she's not here," Sadie shook her head, "And believe me, this isn't how I wanted you to find out. But it's . . . complicated. There just isn't a way around it, I'm afraid."

"What do you mean 'complicated'?" Their father's voice was controlled, but he looked furious. Ellie didn't need heightened empathy to read the signs. His brow was furrowed until his eyebrows squished together, making them look like a whole family of caterpillars. His mouth stretched into a thin, straight line. His cheeks were flushed just like Parker's. And he was crossing his arms over his chest. "For six years, we've been led to believe that Ginny died in an accident. There was a whole story! Then one night you show up and say it was all a lie. What could be more complicated than that?"

"She's alive," Sadie repeated, "but she needs our help."

"What kind of help?" Their dad rattled off a series of rapid-fire questions. "How can this be? They told us she was dead! And now you're telling me the opposite? Is she *okay*? Is she hurt? Why hasn't she contacted me—us—*anyone*?"

Sadie looked uneasy. "From what I understand, she was forced into making some difficult decisions, both for her protection and yours," Sadie continued. "But I think she'd like to be the one to explain things, once she's safe and sound." She paused before adding, "I can tell you that she didn't want to leave you. Any of you."

At that, their dad deflated. Ellie could practically see the anger draining from his body in one giant rush.

"What's wrong with her?" It was Parker's voice, bold and brave, that broke the silence.

"She's trapped, so to speak."

"So to speak." Their dad sounded resigned. "Well, then, you'd better come in for the night," he told Sadie. "It sounds like we have a lot to discuss."

A few minutes later, they were all seated in the living room: Ellie and Dad on the sofa, Parker cross-legged in the vintage wicker peacock chair; Sadie balanced primly at the edge of the rocker. Ellie squished deeper into the worn couch cushions, her knees tucked into her chest. Her body pulsed with electricity as though she'd just run a mile or downed a sugary soda in one gulp. She wondered if this was how Parker felt all the time.

Ellie could tell her dad wasn't quite sure if he believed Sadie. He wore the same expression he'd directed at Ellie the time she tried to blame the C on her science project on her fish, Walter's, stage fright, or at Parker whenever she tried to insist that she *had* brushed her teeth before bed even though the toothbrush was dry (that one happened *a lot*).

"Look, I know it's a lot to process. And I can't explain everything, because I don't have all the answers," Sadie held her palms up in a sign of surrender. "But there really isn't a lot to know at this point, other than that she's in danger." The way Sadie pronounced the word *danger* made Ellie startle. The Danger was what Mabel and George had called the mysterious, hazy, ever-shifting . . . *creature* of sorts that had attacked her and Parker back at Haven. Ellie could tell by Parker's sudden stillness that her sister was thinking the same thing. "The bottom line is she needs to be rescued. That's why I'm here."

Their dad stared silently at Sadie for a moment, then looked at Ellie next to him, then at Parker hunkered in the elaborate wicker chair. He sighed heavily.

"I'm sorry, but given everything that's happened lately, I can't just take you at your word," he told Sadie. "We'll need proof."

Sadie sighed. "I expected as much."

She shuffled in her pocketbook, pulling out a wad of crumbled paper, followed by an uncapped, partially smooshed lipstick in a rather shocking shade of fuchsia. Parker raised her eyebrows at Ellie. *Doesn't inspire much confidence*, Ellie heard her think.

"Ah! There." Sadie withdrew an object from the bottom of her purse. She smiled, apparently relieved. "She sent this." Sadie opened her palm to reveal a silver bracelet, identical to Parker's and Ellie's.

Parker scoffed. "That could be any silver bracelet," she said. "Who's to say you didn't get a replica?"

"Try it on," Sadie urged gently. She extended her hand toward Parker, then Ellie, when Parker refused. In a very un-Ellie-like gesture, she reached out and plucked the bracelet from Sadie's palm, then slipped it on her wrist.

Immediately her body was filled with a warm sensation, not unlike idling on a sandy beach or sipping hot cocoa under a pile of blankets. The bracelet felt like a hug.

It's the feeling of Mom, she thought at Parker. *She's telling the truth.*

Ellie didn't want to take the bracelet off her wrist—she wanted to hold on to this feeling forever. But Parker needed to understand. So, Ellie reluctantly slipped it off and handed it to her sister.

Ellie could see exactly when the feeling struck Parker. Her eyes widened in wonder as her face took on a rosy glow. As the twin typically more attuned to feelings, Ellie was relieved that the bracelet was strong enough for Parker to sense too.

After a moment, Sadie tapped Parker on the wrist.

"Your mom's energy is limited," she told the girls. "She could only funnel so much into the bracelet. Perhaps we give your dad a chance?"

Parker nodded. She removed the bracelet and handed it to her father, who cupped it between his hands as it was too small to encircle his wrist. Ellie and Parker stared as their dad's eyes pricked with tears. The bracelet began to glow a little, like a stubborn ember that won't go out even after a campfire is extinguished. It brightened, turning a shade of orange-red, but their dad didn't flinch. Then, just as the bracelet reached its brightest point, the glow abruptly extinguished.

"I can't feel her anymore," their dad said, staring at the ordinary metal chain in his hands.

"But just think, if we're able to help her, the next time you feel her energy it'll be in person." Sadie's voice was resolute. "The girls' role will be pivotal."

"You need *our* help?!" Parker exclaimed, and Ellie could feel her excitement. It felt like a bee box full of honey or a fireworks show with live rock music. It felt . . . like a lot.

Ellie, on the other hand, was rooted to the sofa, unsure

of what to feel or think at all. Of course she wanted to see her mother, there was no question about that. But that was a chapter of her life that had been written. It had ended—not a happy ending, but an ending she'd thought was final—and everyone had dealt with it and learned to move on to the rest of the book. But now someone was standing in her home telling her that chapter was wrong. Suddenly, nothing was final. And the whole book would have to be rewritten.

"Yes," Sadie answered, rising to place a hand on Parker's shoulder. "I would love your help. If you're willing." She looked past Parker and locked eyes with Ellie. "I know this is quite a shock."

For a split second, Ellie wondered if Sadie could intuit her thoughts the same way she could hear Parker and the animals. But Parker's boisterous interjections distracted her from that train of thought.

"Honestly, it's not that shocking to me!" her sister announced with pride. "I've always said this, but no one listened. I never bought into that whole story. I've known this whole time she was alive." At this, Ellie noticed that Arlo cocked his head skeptically.

Oh, is that so? Ellie heard him think, before settling his chin on his paws.

"Okay, so what's the plan?" Parker wanted to know.

"Slow down, Parker," their dad warned.

"The most important thing we can do right now is finish your training," Sadie said.

"*More* training?" Parker groaned in disbelief. "But that will take too long! We need to help Mom *now*—"

"Excuse me, I haven't said whether you can go anywhere at all," their dad interrupted, raising his voice over Parker's, which put him squarely into Dad Voice territory. They rarely heard their dad use his Dad Voice. Ellie knew this had to be just as overwhelming and confusing for him as it was for her—if not even more.

"Dad . . ." Parker pleaded, her tone tinged with a childish whine that was usually reserved for outfits she wanted at the mall or extra phone time with her friend Clara. Ellie thought it was either very brave or very stupid to employ whining in response to Dad Voice. Likely both.

He sighed again, this time in frustration.

"Let's discuss this over a snack, okay?" he said.

Parker and Ellie exchanged a look. Classic Dad. One of his favorite Dad-isms was, *When the going gets stressful, get some food for thought.* Nevertheless, Ellie's stomach rumbled. Everyone followed him into the kitchen, where he gestured toward the breakfast nook.

Sadie nodded and took a seat at the table, with Parker close behind. Ellie slid onto a cushioned bench, and Arlo settled at her feet beneath the table. Her dad placed a hand on her shoulder, squeezing it comfortingly as he studied her face.

"You okay, L-Bean?" he asked softly.

Ellie shrugged. "I don't know."

He tucked an unruly strand of dark hair behind her ear. It popped right back out, as they always did. "You know," he said, in his most reassuring tone, "you don't have to do anything you don't want to do."

Ellie shook her head. "It doesn't feel like that's an option anymore. I need to do what's right."

He smiled at her, but his eyes were full of sadness. "Oh, Ellie. You're *just* like her," he said. "She once told me that exact same thing. I see so much of her in both of you."

He wrapped one lanky arm around Ellie and the other around Parker and pulled them in close. Ellie thought she might cry. In the warmth and safety of her dad's hugs, she usually let everything out. But in her confusion, all that came was a single tear.

"I guess you could say that with great power comes great—"

"Ew, Dad." Parker's voice was muffled but audible. "You are not going to quote Spider-Man right now, are you?"

Sadie watched with amusement, and their dad chuckled as he released them both.

"Okay," he said, meeting Sadie's eyes across the table. "Tell us more about this training."

CHAPTER TWO

Parker felt victorious. She had been right all along. She had always known that whole "fin-whale-scuba-diving" story about their mom's supposed death was a giant load of baloney. Their mom *didn't* abandon them. *And now,* she and Ellie would get to help RESCUE her!

The more Sadie talked, the better Parker felt. An electric current buzzed under her skin. She felt so light, she thought she might float up to the ceiling like one of the shiny balloons Clara had put in her locker just a few weeks ago for her twelfth birthday. What a roller coaster *that* day had been. She remembered how she'd complained when all those decisions about going to Haven were being made *for* her, not *by* her. At the time, she had thought twelve was going to suck.

Well, she'd been wrong. Twelve was awesome. Twelve was *her* year. Parker had *powers*, and she was going to use them to bring their mom back.

Across from her, Sadie began to describe the additional training she wanted the girls to do. Parker's dad poured glasses of water for everyone and popped some toast in the toaster for Elvis sandwiches. Parker wished they had sodas too, but she knew there was no way he'd let her have sugar at this time of night. As it was, her foot bounced against the floor and she had to clasp her fingers together to keep from tapping them on the place mat in front of her.

"I have no doubt you girls gained a great deal of knowledge from Aunt Mabel and Uncle George during your time at Haven, whether you know it or not. The fact that you were able to rescue your father and an entire train full of people from falling into that canyon certainly proves that. From what I've heard of the incident, you're both extremely capable of harnessing your powers," Sadie said. "But rescuing your mother will require a level of preparedness, knowledge, and finesse that only a more thorough, well-rounded training approach can provide."

Parker remembered the incident like it had just happened—because it *had* just happened! Surviving Mabel's stormy onslaught on Haven House and saving their father and all those train passengers ... she could still feel the last bit of adrenaline tickling her bones and warming her hands as it finished its racecourse through her veins. But she had watched enough superhero shows to know that when someone (especially someone you loved) needed rescuing, you didn't chitchat about it, no matter how daunting or exciting it was. You went IMMEDIATELY. Shouldn't they do the same for their mother?

Like on that one show—the one with the little classroom pets? she wondered. *There was a duckling, or something—weird pet for a classroom—*

"Wonder Pets," Ellie whispered out of the corner of her mouth. "Quit spiraling and listen. This is important." Parker rolled her eyes. Ellie's ability to hear her thoughts could be both useful and annoying. Right now it was the latter.

"Hmm?" Sadie shot them a look like a teacher who'd caught them chatting in class.

"I was just telling Parker this sounds important," Ellie said.

"It is important," Sadie replied. "You can't join the mission to save your mother until I know you're ready, but there isn't time to waste."

Parker loved the word *mission*. It was so official, like a spy. She had also watched a lot of spy shows, and her favorite graphic novel series was about a girl who played on an international soccer team while simultaneously doing undercover work for the FBI and a bunch of European intelligence agencies. *Greta Mystique, Undercover Kicker.*

Ellie's bare toes made contact with Parker's shin under the table. "Ow!" Parker gasped.

"What is going on over there?" Now it was their dad's turn to look annoyed.

"Ellie kicked me," Parker said, then quickly added, "by accident."

She looked over at her sister, who glared back at her with stern eyes.

Pay attention, Ellie mouthed, then she turned back to face Sadie.

How ironic, Ellie telling Parker to pay attention! Ellie was usually the one with her head in the clouds. Parker took a bite of peanut butter–banana goodness and a gulp of water, then put all of her focus on her aunt. "Okay, so are *you* going to train us?"

"Well, no," Sadie explained. "Not really. I'll be around to keep an eye on you, but my training days are behind me. There's an entire branch of the Sentry dedicated to a safe, thorough training experience for young members to gain confidence in their powers."

"The *Sentry*?" Parker echoed.

Now she felt like a spy *and* a superhero. This just kept getting better.

"Yes. I suppose Mabel was too busy concocting nefarious schemes to tell you about your future institution," Sadie said, her frustration creeping into her tone.

"*If* that's what they choose," their dad broke in.

"Wait, you knew about this too?" Parker asked him.

"Of course. Your mother was a member of the Sentry," he said. "She went on many missions to help people, animals, and the planet, both before and after you were born."

"A member?" Sadie scoffed. "Edward, Ginny was top brass. She ran the training camp before the girls were born and maintained a heavy hand in Sentry leadership after their birth. And when she comes back, she'll be in charge again, I'm sure of it."

"*If* she wants to," their dad said again, this time with a polite smile directed at Sadie.

"Of course," Sadie said, smiling politely back. She took a sip of her water and cleared her throat. "Sentry training takes place at the Sentry Mission Control base near Granite, Colorado. They call it Mountain Harbor."

"There's no harbor in the Rockies," Ellie pointed out. "At least, none that I know of." Parker looked at her, noticing for the first time that her twin didn't seem to radiate with the same level of excitement that Parker felt.

"The word 'harbor' as we use it today, the definition you're most used to seeing since you reside in Harborville, usually refers to a coastal area where the water is relatively calm or safe," Sadie explained.

Geez, Parker thought, *she sounds like a walking dictionary.*

"However, before it was applied to nautical refuges," Sadie continued, "the word 'harbor' simply meant a shelter or place of protection."

"Like a haven?" Ellie asked.

"Exactly," Sadie replied.

Parker couldn't help but snort. Ellie's big toe rammed into her leg again.

"What?" Parker snapped. "You don't find it a little ironic that Haven was supposed to be a *safe* place?"

"It was safe," Ellie muttered, "from some things. Like the Danger. It was only when we left Haven that the Danger could reach us."

"Well, it wasn't safe from Mabel," Parker grumbled. She shuddered as the crystal-clear image of her great-aunt, with electric eyes and sparks erupting from her skin, filled her mind. It was still hard to believe that Mabel had tried to *destroy* her—and had succeeded in destroying her own brother, the girls' Great-Uncle George.

"Look," their dad addressed Aunt Sadie. "We should all get some rest. It's been an exhausting day. We can plan with clearer heads in the morning. We have a pullout sofa bed in the study, Sadie. I'll get you fresh sheets."

Sadie's hands snaked across the table, until each clasped Ellie's and Parker's hands. The skin on Parker's arm prickled.

"What happened to you girls at Haven was unimaginable," Sadie said softly. "I will feel guilty for the rest of my life knowing that my family—*our* family—put you through that awful ordeal. But Mabel is gone. And Mountain Harbor *is* safe. You'll be surrounded by some of the most powerful and capable Sentry members as you become more powerful and capable yourselves. It's the safest place you could be."

Sadie's eyes went pink at the rims and glossed over with a tearful sheen. She squeezed the girls' hands tightly in hers.

"And I'll be there the whole time," she assured them. "With you, watching out for you."

Parker swallowed hard and nodded. "So, when do we start?" she asked.

"As soon as you'd like. *If* your dad gives his permission," Sadie replied.

Everyone looked at him, perched by the fridge with a bottle of root beer in his hand (not fair that adults get soda whenever they want, Parker noted). His eyes had that same tearful sheen.

"I could never refuse your mother when she was here," he said after a moment of silence. "And I suppose I'm in no position to refuse her now."

Sadie nodded. "This is the only way for her to come back to you, to be a family again."

"I trust you girls to be safe, behave, and listen to your Aunt Sadie." His voice cracked as he added, "And to bring back your mother."

Parker jumped out of her chair and launched herself at him, squeezing him in the tightest hug she could manage. He ruffled her hair and laughed, then set down his root beer and hugged her back even tighter.

"We will, Dad," Parker said with the side of her face planted against his torso, so her voice sounded strange and muffled inside her own head.

"I'm counting on it," he said.

"There's a flight to Denver at ten in the morning that still has seats available," Sadie announced, already scrolling on her phone. "Should I book it?"

Parker pulled away and looked up at her dad's face. He stared down at her, then looked over Parker's head at Ellie at the table.

"Yes! Book it! I want to go!" Parker said, hopping with excitement.

Her dad laughed. "Yes, I think we all figured that. But what about Ellie?"

Parker turned around and surveyed her sister, a slouchy, frizz-haired ragdoll in sunshine yellow pajamas. She wished she could read Ellie's mind like Ellie could kind of read hers.

Ellie regarded them all for a few long, torturous moments. Finally, she sighed. "Are there animals at this place?"

Sadie smiled an impossibly wide, toothpaste commercial smile. "You sound just like your mother."

"That's what everyone keeps saying," Ellie mumbled, tucking her chin in embarrassment.

"Yes, they have a few camp pets, so to speak," Sadie said. "Plus all the local wildlife. Deer, elk, raccoons, martens, eagles—oh! When I was there, we had these two black bear cubs that came every day because they could smell the berry bushes in our greenhouse. Cutest little guys. Your mom had to talk them down from their tantrums when they realized they weren't going to get any berries. On the last day of camp, I took them each a handful of every berry we grew. I still have a Polaroid of their faces totally covered with berry juice."

"That's adorable," Ellie said, looking interested for the first time all night. She took a deep breath and blew it out. "All right," she said, prompting Parker to grin from ear to ear. "Let's go."

"Do you think they'll give us cool *uniforms* at the camp?" Parker asked, holding up a pair of the overalls they'd been given at Haven. "I guess I don't need to pack these, huh?"

"You do love your uniforms, don't you?" Ellie laughed.

"Well, duh! Uniforms are awesome! They look cool and they make you a team! Especially tight, stretchy type uniforms," Parker said. "Like superheroes wear. With patterns on them, or logos—like tiger claw marks, or thunderbolts! Then you're really intimidating."

"You've thought about uniforms a lot, haven't you?"

Parker pulled her little notebook from its spot in the book stack next to her bed and flipped it open to page fifty-six. Her *Careers* list. She held it up, tapping her finger on "Uniform Designer," an entry near the top of the list, sandwiched between "Museum Curator" and "Cereal Taste-Tester."

"Hey, you want to work in a museum too?" Ellie asked. "I've always wanted to work in a museum."

"I didn't know that," Parker said. "What would you want to do?"

"I always thought it would be fun to create the animal dioramas," Ellie replied, folding a T-shirt and gently placing it into her duffel. "What about you?"

"Geology displays, for sure," Parker said. "Remember that one museum Mom and Dad took us to that had that whole room that was like an amethyst cave?"

"Yes! It was like walking into a giant geode," Ellie said with a nod. "It was incredible, like a cave made of crystals. But we were so little then. I bet it wouldn't seem that big now."

"It's one of my clearest memories of Mom," Parker said, closing the notebook and tossing it into her bag. A smile crept across her face as she let the memory fill her head. "I remember I was in total awe. I couldn't stop smiling, and I looked up at her, and she was just watching us with her own giant grin.

And I couldn't believe that she found *us* more exciting than that huge crystal cave, but she did. All this time, it never made sense to me how she could leave us if she felt that way.

"But," Parker continued as she tossed a handful of clean undergarments into her bag, "now we know she didn't have a choice. She was in danger."

Ellie sighed. "Parker, of course we need to rescue her, but aren't you worried? What if the danger she's in is *the* Danger? Doesn't that scare you, especially after everything we just went through?"

Parker thought about it for a moment, then shrugged and shook her head. "No, I'm not really worried," she declared. "Are you?"

Ellie didn't answer, keeping her eyes trained on her duffel bag.

"Ellie . . ." Parker said, as sympathetically as she could manage, given her excitement about their new adventure. She crossed the room to sit down next to her sister. "I get it. And it's totally okay to feel that way."

"You're just saying that," Ellie mumbled.

"No," Parker said, "it makes perfect sense why you're afraid. And if I weren't so excited right now, I'd probably feel worried too. But what happened at Haven is not going to happen to us again."

"How do you know?" Ellie questioned. "Everyone always says how powerful Mom was. If she's in a situation that even she can't get out of, how are we supposed to go up against it?"

"One step at a time. First we go to Sentry camp. Dad wouldn't let us go if he didn't think it was a good idea."

Ellie sighed, then finally met Parker's gaze. "You're not usually this optimistic."

"You're not usually this cautious," Parker replied, one corner of her lips tugging upward. "We've both learned a lot from each other this summer, huh, sis?"

A grin crept across Ellie's face too as she nodded slowly. "Yes, I guess we have."

"That's the other reason I know we're going to be fine," Parker said. She reached over and grabbed both of Ellie's clasped hands in hers. "We're a team. If we stick together, nothing can stop us, right?"

"Right," Ellie said, her grin widening to a smile. "So, does our sister team have uniforms, or what?"

"Ellie," Parker said mock-indignantly, "did you not get enough of the 'twins wearing matching clothes' thing when we were little?"

"I'm just saying, if we're going to be unstoppable, maybe we need Parker McFadden–designed, super-stretchy uniforms," Ellie said.

"With pockets!" Parker added.

"Lots of pockets," Ellie agreed. "And utility belts."

"Well, I do know one thing we both have in our possession that basically has built-in utility storage," Parker joked. She reached over to the pile of clothes she would not be taking to Mountain Harbor and held up a pair of the offending overalls. "*Not* an original Parker McFadden design."

They doubled over laughing until their dad rapped on the door and declared, "Lights out!"

CHAPTER THREE

Goodbyes at the San Francisco airport the next morning were misty-eyed but short.

"Call me later tonight," Dad said, as he squeezed them both one final time. "Keep me updated on everything, even if you think it isn't important. When you find Mom . . ." he swallowed. "Tell her I love her. And that I've missed her. And that I can't wait to see her." He kissed them each on the forehead. "I'll see you very soon," he said, seemingly more for his own sake than for theirs. "Love you bunches. Be safe. Have fun!"

"We will," Parker said, sounding quite sure of it.

Ellie wished she felt the same. But three hours later, as she exited the plane bound for their mysterious new chapter, she couldn't shake the feeling that the last thing they were going to do at this camp was "have fun."

Parker practically skipped through the terminal at Sadie's side, her purple backpack flopping against her body with every bouncy step. Ellie hung back, scanning each and every sign to make sure they were heading the right way. The woman who had checked them in in San Francisco had written instructions to pick up Arlo on a little piece of notepad paper and given it to Ellie, who was obviously the most nervous about the prospect.

Until recently, Arlo had spent his whole life roaming free all over Haven, sniffing and running and even peeing wherever he liked. Something seemed wrong about fencing him in, never mind loading him into a kennel and onto the bottom of a plane. But there wasn't an alternative. Haven House was gone, and so were Uncle George and Aunt Mabel, who had cared for him since puppyhood.

Deep down, Ellie was overjoyed that Arlo got to come. In the roller coaster that had been this summer, he'd been her unexpected rock. She couldn't imagine embarking on the second half of this wild journey without him. But she felt a twinge of guilt every time she pictured him rolling away in his hard plastic crate. What did he think was happening? Would he be scared? Or was this just another job to him, another leg of this unfolding adventure?

She picked up her pace, not wanting to wait a moment longer to retrieve him. She kept looking for the signs for— she consulted the note from the woman in San Francisco— "excess baggage pickup." But as she neared Sadie and Parker, her eagle-eyed focus faltered a bit.

"So, it *was* the Danger?" she heard Parker mutter, softly enough that Ellie almost wasn't sure she'd heard correctly over the din of the nearby food court.

"Definitely," Sadie answered. "I was lucky . . . It nearly got me. I don't know how I got away."

Ellie's heart flipped uncomfortably.

"And Ginny, well, she just vanished. At first, I had hope. I looked for days, then weeks, then months. But there was no sign of her anywhere. Eventually, I had to accept that must be it. By then, the higher-ups at the Sentry had already told your father the *story*."

Parker snorted. "*That* story," she scoffed. "Fin whales and scuba diving. *So* not convincing. The Sentry needs help inventing their cover stories. I knew that was bogus when I was seven."

Sadie laughed out loud, a bright, jubilant, bell peal of a laugh that seemed to overtake the entire terminal.

So far, Ellie thought traveling with Sadie had been a pleasure. Their dad tended to get frazzled on trips—once, while visiting Memaw and Grandad McFadden, he'd nearly exited the Chicago airport without any of their checked luggage. But Sadie was not an adult who needed help staying on track. With her tight bun, fancy-looking black slacks, matching blazer with an expensive-looking crystal flamingo pin in the lapel, ruffled white top, and shiny black patent high heels,

Ellie figured that anyone seeing their trio might assume that she and Parker had traveled unaccompanied and that Sadie was an airline employee transporting them to their final destination. Their aunt looked like maybe she *ran* the whole airport. All she needed was a walkie-talkie and a lanyard with her security card on it.

They descended the escalator into the hive of people and luggage that was baggage claim. Ellie's eyes immediately surveyed the walls for the excess baggage pickup sign, but she didn't have to look too hard. Just past two of the baggage carousels, she spotted a small crescent of beige plastic crates, each containing a different animal.

As she moved toward the crates, one of them shook so violently that she thought for sure it would tip on its side. A shrieking yowl rang out through the massive hall, so loud and earsplitting it seemed like it had come from a pterodactyl rather than whatever was inside that crate.

That orange cat cried the whole way, she heard Arlo's voice nearby. *Very upset. So dramatic! Got a lot of attention but nothing helped. Needs professional help, if you ask me.*

"Tough luck," Ellie muttered, almost inaudible to humans, but loud enough for Arlo's sensitive ears to hear. "We had a baby up top that started to cry. It seems like everyone is sensitive today."

Ellie knelt down next to the shaking crate, feeling the poor cat's fear and anger coursing through her own body. Peering into the shadowy crate, she saw an orange tabby, hair standing on end, like a Halloween decoration or a cartoon cat that had been electrocuted by some crafty mouse. The tabby hissed as Ellie rested her hand on top of the crate, then he let out another angry scream of a meow.

Out! Out! Out! She heard the cat's frantic voice in her head as its audible scream rang out above the hubbub of the baggage claim area. *Trapped! Loud! Small! Bad! Where is toy mouse? Where is bed? Where is people? Out!*

"I can't let you out," Ellie whispered, hoping the cat understood. Its wide amber eyes darted back and forth between her and the busy, foreign room. "You have to wait for your human. It's too busy here. You'll get lost, or hurt. But I promise someone will help you soon."

Ellie slipped her hand between the thin metal bars of the crate door and took a deep breath. Closing her eyes, she let calm fill her, replacing the cat's panic and fear. Soft fur pressed against her knuckles, tickling between her fingers, as she channeled the serene energy from herself to the tabby.

"Is this your cat?" asked a baggage attendant as he emerged from the excess baggage room with someone's mountain bike.

"Uh, no," Ellie said, "this dog is mine." She tilted her head to her left where Arlo lay calmly with his paws straight out in front of him, poking through the slats of the kennel door. "I just love cats, um, especially orange tabbies."

"Looks like orange tabbies love you," the attendant said with an impressed grin. "Henley here has been yowling like a banshee since we unloaded him. Probably since San Fran, if I had to guess."

Good guess, Arlo thought, the sentiment dripping with sarcasm. *You must be psychic.* Apparently being stuck in a crate had made him sassier.

"Henley," Ellie cooed, rubbing the cat's side with her knuckles. "Nice to meet you."

Thank you. Pleasure's all mine, came his response.

Sadie's high heels and voice sounded behind Ellie.

"How'd he do?" Sadie asked the attendant who, Ellie noticed upon standing, wore a nametag that read *Robin*.

"The cattle dog?" Robin asked. "Perfect customer, as far as I've seen."

Ellie sighed in relief. Sadie smiled at her, then handed Robin the voucher they'd been given to claim Arlo. "Thank you," she said.

"I should be thanking your kid here," Robin said as he wheeled a flat over for them. "Seems like she's some sort of cat whisperer."

"Oh, she's my niece," Sadie corrected, placing a hand on Ellie's shoulder. "And yes, she's very talented like that."

"I hope someone in your family is saving up for vet school, that's all I'm saying," Robin said with a chuckle. "You ladies have a great time in the Mile High City, ya hear?" He tapped the top of Arlo's crate and went back to work, disappearing into the excess baggage room.

"Just like your mom," Sadie murmured to Ellie with a grin.

Ellie couldn't help but grin back.

Ellie nearly made herself carsick staring out the window of the rental car's back seat (Parker had called shotgun as soon as they'd set foot to pavement). She watched as the amber plains turned to a bustling city and the city turned to rolling green foothills that finally gave way to craggy rock faces and a sea of endless evergreens.

They drove through a few ski towns, full of people pursuing outdoorsy activities. Seemingly all the cars had kayaks or bikes on top. Cyclists whizzed down every street as they worked their way through a small town that reminded her a little bit of Bearsted, where Haven was located. But instead of antiques and vintage clothing, here the shops sold bike gear and ski equipment and were interspersed with cafes and hip-looking restaurants with patios full of helmet-wearing grown-ups drinking fizzy drinks and sharing pizzas.

A few more switchbacks up the mountain, a few more pops of Ellie's ears, a few more songs on the radio, and Sadie pulled off the road into what appeared to be a gravel parking lot for a trailhead. She parked the car between two others and shut off the engine. Then she opened the trunk and reached into her black-and-white striped tote bag, extracting a pair of sneakers, which she proceeded to change into. She carefully stowed the shiny high heels in the bag.

"Ready to walk?" she asked, turning back to Ellie and Arlo.

Arlo jumped to all fours immediately, tail wagging and tongue flopping.

"I guess so!" Ellie laughed.

They unloaded their duffels from the trunk, strapping them over their shoulders. Laden with her backpack and her duffel, staring at the rocky trail in front of her that disappeared into a thick maze of brush and gnarled birch trees, Ellie wished she'd packed *much* lighter than she had.

Once they started their trek, however, the last thing on Ellie's mind was the weight of her load. A rainbow assortment of wildflowers revealed itself around every corner. Tiny butterflies in pale blues and creamy yellows fluttered up in a dainty cyclone every time one of them brushed against a bush with a foot or an elbow. Arlo managed to chase three chipmunks up a tree; the smile on his face was bigger than Ellie had ever seen before.

They passed a small creek where Ellie was pleased to spot a little brown weasel on the banks, washing its face in the water.

"Pine marten," Sadie said. "Very common around here. They usually come out at night, but it must have wanted an early dinner."

A few short minutes after the creek, they came to a fork in the trail, and Sadie led them up the steeper offshoot. Ellie's thighs burned as they hiked up what was practically a staircase of boulders. Just as Ellie thought she couldn't haul herself any further, they reached the last rocky step and she found herself looking out over a bright meadow carpeted in azure columbine and circled by towering spruce. She gasped in awe of the picture-perfectness as the warm sun hit her cheeks.

"Holy crap," Parker uttered.

"That's what I said too, the first time I saw it," Sadie remarked. "Come on, we're right up here." She gestured to an outcropping of smooth boulders to their right, butted against a slightly sloping hill. A rather rotund marmot chittered at them as they neared, then scurried into a crevice at the back of the boulder pile.

"Here we are," Sadie said. She patted a large boulder at

the front of the outcrop with a level of fondness that even Ellie, proud owner of several solid minerals of the companion variety, found odd.

"It's a pile of rocks," Parker remarked, unimpressed.

"Well, this isn't *all* of it," Sadie explained. "We try to keep the entrances pretty lowkey, since NORAD is only about a hundred miles away."

"What's NORAD?" Ellie asked, her face squinting, not only from confusion but also against the bright mountain sun.

"North American Aerospace Defense Command," Parker rattled off with a brisk ease.

"How did you know that?" Ellie questioned.

"Don't make me get out the Career List notebook," Parker said. "It's at the bottom of my duffel."

"Anyway," Sadie interrupted, pulling the girls back to the topic at hand, "I brought you to this entrance because I helped build it. Everyone who comes to Mountain Harbor gets to add on."

"Sounds like Haven House," Ellie pointed out.

"Exactly," Sadie said. "And we do that for a reason. When we move something into place with our powers, like a boulder or a trunk or a thick vine, or, yes, even an old ironing board or a deflated basketball, we imbue it with a shard of our energy. Over time, all those little bits of energy accumulate into a very powerful shield, almost like a magnetic field, that helps protect against danger."

"Danger, or *the* Danger?" Parker asked.

"Both," Sadie answered, her voice grave.

"Just like the stone wall at Haven!" Ellie blurted out, remembering.

"Yes, that was built in this manner," Sadie said, nodding. "Stone by stone, placed not with bare hands but with magic. Lots of small stones make a very powerful wall."

Ellie and Parker watched as a small, round boulder floated up from a patch of soil and fluttered over the top of the outcrop, as if it were one of the dainty blue butterflies, finally settling in a nook between two large boulders.

They were so enthralled watching Sadie maneuver the rock that they didn't even notice the woman who had emerged from the boulder field.

"Sadie Powers," the woman said, sounding not at all pleased to see the person who went along with that name. "You're just about the last person I thought I'd see here."

CHAPTER FOUR

Michelle," Sadie said, her lips tight. Parker watched Sadie's shoulders tense as she turned to face the woman.

"Director Moreau," the woman corrected, her tone cool.

"*Co*-Director Moreau," Sadie replied, holding up a finger and smiling.

Michelle Moreau was a tall Black woman (dressed from head to toe in form-fitting steel gray, which Parker hoped was a uniform) with long, precisely waved hair cascading over her shoulders. Parker thought there was something familiar about her face, with its striking combination of round cheeks on prominent cheekbones. Her deep brown eyes peered from behind thick, black-framed glasses, surveying everything around her with the intensity of a bird of prey.

"Your sister has been gone for six years," Moreau said, "and you've been an absentee member for twice that. The newer Sentry members don't even know who the Powers sisters are."

"Well, they're going to now," Sadie declared. She called the twins forward with a dramatic arm gesture. Arlo trotted forward in such near-perfect form that he looked to Parker like he was competing in some kind of fancy dog show.

"Yes, I see you've brought your nieces, which is why I'm keeping this meeting as professional as possible," Moreau said. She seemed calm and collected, but Parker could see her eyes narrow every time she looked at Sadie.

What in the world happened between these two? Parker thought, directing her musing toward her sister. Out of the corner of her eye, she saw Ellie shrug inconspicuously in response.

"I'll accept the girls for training, even though summer session is already halfway through," Moreau stated. "I know they received some previous instruction . . ." She trailed off, as if she wasn't sure what else she could say in front of them. She clicked her tongue, crossed her arms, and finally settled on, "Well, we all know how that went."

"*They* do," Sadie said, letting a brisker tone take over. "I'm not sure how you know what they went through."

"I had eyes on the situation," Moreau replied.

What?! So there *were* people spying on them? A shiver ran up Parker's spine, though she couldn't tell if it was because she found that idea weird or awesome.

"Of course," Sadie scoffed. "You sent Barb, didn't you?"

"I didn't send Barb, Sadie," Moreau clarified with sharpness. "She volunteered. She hasn't wanted to spend more than a day at this base in years. Too many reminders of the woman who abandoned her."

Moreau's words were ice now. Parker shivered again. This conversation was suddenly starting to sound like the soap operas she sometimes caught Trudy, their retired neighbor and occasional babysitter, watching on her tablet while Parker and Ellie did their homework.

"I thought we were keeping this conversation professional," Sadie hissed.

"Oh trust me, I am, Powers," Moreau said. "If it weren't, I'd have a much different set of words to say to the woman who disappeared and left my beautiful, sweet sister without so much as a goodbye."

"Michelle—" Sadie started, but Moreau held up a silencing hand and cut her off.

"And as far as work is concerned, I sent you on an assignment to Lake Natron years ago, and you stopped reporting six weeks in, so *professionally* I have reason to be upset."

Sadie sighed. "It was complicated."

"I'm sure it was," Moreau said dismissively. "Now, if you don't mind, I'd love to get the girls settled. I'm sure you have somewhere to *disappear* to."

Parker looked at Ellie. *Oh, man, this is just like Trudy's soap opera . . .*

"Michelle," Sadie said, "you know I'm not letting these girls stay here without me. Not after everything they just went through."

"Fine," Moreau sighed. "But I am going to make you work, Powers. As you know, everyone here earns their place. Think you can handle that without running off?"

"Of course, *Director*."

Parker got a better look at Moreau as they walked past her. Moreau returned her gaze, and something tickled the back of Parker's brain as the director's sharp eyes bored into her.

"Boudin!" Parker blurted out as the realization washed over her. The sister, this "Barb" who was sent to watch them in Haven, had to be none other than Ms. Boudin, the helpful librarian. Parker knew she had seen these exact eyes before. Ms. Boudin and Moreau must be . . . *twins*.

"Watch your step," Moreau called as Ellie and Arlo, up in front, reached the top of a stone staircase. From there, the steps began to slope downward as far as Parker could see. They trudged slowly, step after step, making their winding, never-ending descent. Even Arlo, usually one to bound down staircases, seemed to be exercising caution.

Parker wondered what waited for them at the eventual conclusion. A medieval-looking castle with rustic furniture and flaming torches? A glass-walled spy lair with computer servers and blinking red lights? Or some underground version of Haven House—an eclectic, mystical amalgamation of everyone who'd ever set foot inside it?

After what could have just as easily been one minute or twenty, the bottom of the staircase finally gave way to a large, open cavern. *Huh*, thought Parker. It didn't look like a castle or a spy lair or even like Haven. In fact, it didn't really look like anything Parker had ever seen. It was rustic like a ski lodge but cozy like a living room. Modern like a nice hotel, but with a nod to nature at every turn. It felt surprising and unexpected but also strangely comfortable, sort of like everything in her weird new life.

"Welcome to Mountain Harbor," Moreau said, as Parker and Ellie stopped to look around. "We call this the Atrium."

Parker scanned the room. To her right, a long row of uniform, hand-carved doors were set in a timber-paneled wall. The doors extended all the way to the back of the chamber, where there appeared to be an archway with another set of steps behind it. To her left, a traditional great room setup took up half of the space. There were comfy sofas strewn with handmade blankets and pillows, a fireplace nestled into the stone, a chess table and a real piano, and houseplants scattered casually around. Ahead of her, the farther part of the space featured a ring of stalactites and stalagmites circling a natural pool of teal-tinged, sparkling water. Parker even caught a glimpse of a few crystals in the walls. The room was lit by lanterns made of twigs and rice paper, swaying from large hooks protruding from solid timber beams.

A little bit of everything, she thought at Ellie.

"I'll say," Ellie murmured.

A dark-haired teenage boy emerged from the archway at the far end of the Atrium. He loped into the room, like some sort of leggy seabird that hadn't yet grown accustomed to its limbs. Everything about him was long and lanky—even lankier than their dad, Parker thought, which was really saying something.

"Everything all right, Director?" he asked, zeroing in on the twins.

"Just fine, Aiden," Moreau answered. "New recruits. In fact, I could use your help. Show them around a bit, please? Ms. Powers and I have some things to straighten out in my office."

"Sure thing!" The boy smiled, revealing a row of perfect, white teeth. Parker wondered if he'd had braces or if he was lucky enough to be born that way.

"Parker and Ellie McFadden, this is Aiden Baxter."

Moreau gently nudged the girls toward their would-be tour guide. Parker felt like a little kid next to his lean, towering frame—he was even taller than Director Moreau. He beamed at them, pushing a tidal wave of unruly midnight black hair off his forehead to reveal two steel gray eyes. Parker had no idea eyes came in that color. They were unlike anything she'd ever seen.

In fact, she noted with no shortage of excitement, his eyes nearly matched his outfit . . . the same granite-colored mock turtleneck jumpsuit that Moreau wore. *Uniforms!*

"Thank you, Aiden," Moreau nodded and took off down a corridor.

"Enjoy the tour! I'll see you in a bit," Sadie added, rushing off after Moreau.

Aiden watched the adults retreat, then turned back to the girls and their dog. Arlo's nose wiggled back and forth, trying to get a definitive scent profile on the new kid in front of him. Ellie patted his head to reassure him.

"So, are you hungry?" Aiden asked. "Afternoon snack is just wrapping up, but everyone should still be hanging around the commissary, and I know there are probably a few premade sandwiches and salads left over from lunch."

"That sounds great," Parker said. She hadn't realized until Aiden mentioned it just how hungry she was after that hike.

"Great!" Aiden replied happily. "You can leave your bags here. We'll grab them later."

They slid their bags off their shoulders as instructed and followed him through the same archway he'd come from, then down another set of steps. (Parker was relieved to find these were relatively straight and much shorter than the last set.) At the base of the stairs, they passed more heavy wooden doors that seemed to lead into log cabin–like rooms, though she couldn't see enough to tell what they were used for. Aiden turned to lead them down a narrow, rocky tunnel with a smooth, colored-glass mosaic floor. The mosaic depicted a thick, flowering vine winding its way around an ancient Roman column. The vine was peppered with red flowers that seemed almost to glow in the shimmering twinkle lights strung along either side of the corridor. Parker thought they looked like rubies.

"Look," Ellie said as they reached the end of the tunnel. She rammed her elbow into Parker's and pointed to the top of the mosaic column. There, rendered in glass, was the same lion symbol as the one atop the weathervane their mother had left them. But the symbol, Parker remembered, was part of a pair. She wondered if there was another mosaic like this one somewhere else at Mountain Harbor, bearing the Earth symbol instead.

They entered yet another chamber lined with more timber-paneled doors, though these seemed like they'd been plopped wherever instead of neatly lined in a row. One door had been painted a bright turquoise, while another was electric purple. Another door was blue and framed with twinkle lights. Multiple doors were adorned with white dry erase boards, which were full of rainbow notes and doodles.

"Live-in bunks," Aiden said. He pointed to a log cabin room with a black door. "Home sweet home."

"You live here all the time?" Parker asked.

"Yep," Aiden replied.

"What about your twin?" Ellie questioned.

Aiden's perfect white smile faltered. "No, not with my twin," he answered. "But of course, there are plenty of twins here. And in a few moments, you can meet all of them."

Through another short tunnel, Aiden flung open a set of tall, wooden double doors. The room they stepped into was alive with the hum of various conversations, but it stopped as soon as Parker and Ellie entered.

Warm blood rushed to Parker's cheeks. She knew they were bright pink, but there was nothing she could do to stop it.

"New recruits!" Aiden announced, gesturing to them with both arms, like a host on a home shopping network.

"In July?" an older teen girl who looked like a carbon copy of Director Moreau asked in disbelief.

"Yes, in July," Aiden replied. "Are you questioning your mother's judgment, Jules?"

"Of course not." She sighed and rolled her eyes, then slid out of her chair and crossed the room with an outstretched hand. "Juliette Moreau. You can call me Jules. Everyone does."

She grabbed Parker's hand and shook it, then took Ellie's and did the same. "If you ever need anything and can't find my mom, you can always come to me or my sister, Len." She gestured back to the table, where a girl who looked very much like Jules waved. "We're sort of like unofficial camp counselors."

Jules wore the same stretchy gray shirt as Aiden, though she had somewhat personalized hers by adding a teal scarf and a crystal brooch. With her tortoiseshell cat-eye glasses, she looked like she was one poodle skirt short of a sock hop. Her vintage style reminded Parker a bit of Barb Boudin— Jules's aunt, she realized. Len, on the other hand, wore a plain hoodie over her gray turtleneck, and her hair was tied up in a messy bun.

"Or . . ." Aiden interrupted. "You can talk to the *actual* counselor, Finn, who you will meet later this afternoon."

"Whatever." Jules waved a dismissive hand at Aiden as if he were a bothersome gnat. "Finn doesn't know where the Twizzlers are stashed." Jules winked at Parker, and Parker grinned back. "Cute dog," she said to Ellie, then returned to her seat.

"Everyone, meet Parker and Ellie," Aiden said, as he continued to walk them through the dining tables.

It was then that Parker saw two very familiar faces, smiling brightly (and identically) at her and Ellie. Casey and Cassie Phillips, the popular twins from Ellie and Parker's school in Harborville! Parker didn't know why she was surprised to see them there, given that she had just glimpsed them at the train disaster a day prior. She had figured they were part of this brand-new world she and Ellie had been thrown into. But nevertheless, she was caught off guard and unsure of what to say.

Thankfully, Casey spoke first.

"We know Parker and Ellie," he said.

"Really?" Jules asked, sounding a bit jealous. Parker couldn't imagine why, although she had been eager to be helpful right off the bat. Maybe Jules was one of those people who loved power and needed to have the upper hand in every social setting, Parker thought. Or maybe she just wanted to befriend the new kid—or in this case, *kids*.

"Yeah, we go to school together," Cassie replied.

"Whoa," said a boy seated next to Cassie. He had a round face and icy blue eyes, topped off with a mop of shaggy blond hair. "Small world, huh?"

"Guess so," Parker replied with a shrug and a nervous chuckle.

Now, THAT boy is CUTE, Parker thought.

Ellie laughed through her nose.

CRAP. She hadn't meant to think it *that* loudly. A fresh round of pink flushed her cheeks.

"I'm Gray Van Loon," the boy said, "and over there is my sister, Gabby." Gabby, who looked a lot like Gray but with a long blond braid, waved reluctantly from her seat near the

Moreau twins. "We're from Chicago. We'll be sophomores this upcoming school year. What grade are you guys in?"

Parker was embarrassed to admit she wasn't in high school yet.

"Seventh," Ellie answered.

Parker's face went hot AGAIN. Curse the amount of blood flow to her face! She clenched her fists and jaw simultaneously.

"I loved seventh grade," Gray remarked, staring wistfully past them as though he were watching movie highlights on a screen behind their heads. "That was the best year. Career fair, chemistry, World History, *A Wrinkle in Time! The Hobbit!*"

With every entry to his list, Gray's excitement grew and grew, to the point that Parker thought he might eject from his seat.

"Okay, calm down, nerdface," Gabby teased. "Maybe they don't love school as much as you do."

"I *love* school," Parker blurted out. And not just to impress Gray. She did love school and hearing him list his favorite parts of seventh grade made her itch to go back.

"All right then," Gabby said with a shrug, "carry on."

"Actually," Aiden cut in, "I think I'd better find some food for our new friends, and I think the rest of you need to go get ready for Botany."

"I was just going to say that," Jules huffed. She shot straight out of her chair with her hands propped on her hips. "C'mon, everyone," she barked, in a way that sounded an awful lot like her mother. "Greenhouse in ten!"

While the rest of the kids trickled out of the mess hall, Aiden rifled through the shelves of a walk-in cooler that had been carved into the cavern wall. He emerged with an armful of wrapped sandwiches.

"Egg salad, hummus and veg, avocado caprese, apple and brie," he listed off.

"Ooh, fancy sandwiches," Parker remarked. "I'll try the apple one."

He handed her the small sandwich parcel, swathed in brown paper and labeled in someone's perfect, flowing script. *Probably Jules's*, Parker thought, since she seemed like a perfectionist who needed to be in charge of everything.

"Hummus for me," Ellie said. "And is there somewhere I can feed Arlo?"

"Of course," Aiden said. "Let's go get your bags and I'll show you to one of our open bunks. Then we'll get you hooked up with some uniforms, and I think I can even get you to the Greenhouse without being too terribly late for your first Botany session!"

Uniforms! Parker squealed in internal excitement. *Finally.*

CHAPTER FIVE

After getting settled in a bunk room and receiving their Sentry clothes—which Ellie knew made Parker happy, though she herself would have preferred her overalls and a T-shirt to the tight mock turtleneck, pants, and hiking boots— the girls followed Aiden through more passages and caverns until they reached a room that caught Ellie completely off guard.

She had wondered, from the moment the Greenhouse was mentioned during lunch, how there could possibly be a greenhouse this far underground. From what she'd seen of it so far, Mountain Harbor seemed to be some kind of extra-large, snaking, subterranean cave. As best as she could fig-ure, any "greenhouse" must involve some sort of UV lights to mimic the sun and help trap heat in the room.

She couldn't have been more wrong.

When Aiden pushed open a glass door and motioned the girls inside, Ellie suddenly found herself bathed in sun-light. *Actual,* glorious sunlight. A half dome of sparkling glass made up the wall opposite the door. Glints and glimmers of the bright afternoon sun were caught inside the glass, like the prism she had in their bedroom at home. The whole thing looked like a giant sunshine net, which, Ellie thought, it kind of was. She had to squint against the white-gold radiance just to get a decent look at the Greenhouse itself.

Every fruit and vegetable that Ellie had ever heard of seemed to be represented. The largest plant appeared to be an apple tree, rooted in a large soil bed near the glass wall and sporting little pinkish-red orbs that dangled from its branches. There were skinny banana trees and robust raspberry shrubs, a raised bed box full of pepper and tomato plants, and a trellis full of petite white blossoms and dangling crescent-shaped beans.

And the flowers! Ellie felt like she'd been transported to a cottage garden somewhere in the English countryside. Tall stalks of hollyhocks in varying shades of violets and pinks stood in a row, like floral soldiers on alert. Tulips, irises, rose bushes, snapdragons, and many more that Ellie couldn't name filled the Greenhouse with their pleasant spectrum of colors and fragrances.

She noticed a lot of other plants too—different grasses, saplings, shrubs, and even weeds graced some of the pots, trays, and beds. There was also an impressive array of herbs in a long box running right along the glass wall. It looked like the McFaddens' little herb box in the kitchen window at home, times a hundred.

"We must be on the side of the mountain?" Parker posited out of the corner of her mouth, mostly at Ellie. "I wonder if there are any other aboveground rooms like this one."

"A couple," Aiden answered. "But not many. We try to keep a low profile."

Parker clicked her tongue. "NORAD, am I right?"

Aiden let out a laugh that was so contagious, it caused Ellie to giggle as well. It sounded like the honking of a goose and the bleat of a sheep and the gleeful cackle of a merry-but-not-at-all-frightening clown. Several heads turned away from their botanical tasks to see what the commotion was. If Aiden was fazed, he didn't seem to notice. "Where'd you learn about that?"

"I know stuff," Parker answered with a casual shrug and head tilt that Ellie immediately recognized as part of Parker's "cool and mysterious" body language.

"Well, yes, we definitely want to stay off of NORAD's radar," Aiden said. His shoulders hunched a bit as he angled toward the girls and dropped his head and voice. "But it's not the *only* reason."

Aiden's "cool and mysterious" body language was *much* better than Parker's, Ellie decided.

"What are the other reasons?" Ellie asked.

But before Aiden could even open his mouth to answer, a voice boomed through the Greenhouse.

"Baxter! You'd better not be planning on keeping those newbies all to yourself!"

Aiden whipped around and stepped out of the way of the girls. "Of course not, Instructor DeSoto. Just, uh, explaining a few things about the Greenhouse. Parker, Ellie, this is Instructor DeSoto. They'll be your teacher for several lessons, your camp counselor whenever you need them, and the leader on most of your missions."

"Please, like I keep telling Baxter here, you can call me Finn," Instructor DeSoto said, maneuvering past a rustic potting table to cross the room toward Parker and Ellie.

Finn had a kind face and a pleasant smile. Ellie thought maybe that was because their mouth was quite wide and their teeth were on the larger side, making their expressions seem especially enthusiastic. They had a thin face with a hawk-like nose, and a tuft of hair styled to spike upward, which also reminded Ellie of a hawk, or maybe a falcon—something with a crown of unruly feathers. Finn's hair, Ellie noticed as they approached, was a shimmery copper in the direct sun and a deep, earthy brown as soon as they stepped out of it. Finn was the only person she'd seen so far who didn't wear the same uniform as everyone else at Mountain Harbor. Their outfit resembled something out of an action movie where the heroes went on an archeological dig in the desert—head-to-toe khaki and brown boots, with a sage green kerchief around their neck.

"Anyway, you're just in time for our lesson," Finn said, ushering Ellie and Parker toward one of the planting tables. "We've just been getting the pots ready."

The twins followed Finn to a planting table in the middle of the Greenhouse. The Sentry teens were all gathered around it, and Gray obligingly shuffled over to make room for Parker and Ellie. At the center of the table sat several small clay pots, and next to the pots were little bundles of what Ellie thought looked like yellow snapdragons.

"Toadflax," Finn announced, skirting around the edges of the potting table. "Also known as *butter and eggs* or *wild snapdragon*."

"They're cute," Gabby remarked, gently pinching one of the blossoms in her fingers.

"They're adorable," Finn agreed. "They're also a huge problem."

"What do you mean?" Gabby asked.

"Toadflax is an invasive species," Finn explained. "In the plant world, we sometimes refer to it as a noxious weed. These species are transported to places that they aren't native to, oftentimes by human trade and travel. Now, in and of itself, that isn't really a problem, unless the species displaces or harms the existing life in the biome.

"For example, our adorable toadflax here finds the foothill prairies and mountain pastures of Colorado a wonderful place to spread out their extensive, powerful root systems," Finn continued, "which makes it difficult for the array of native grasses and wildflowers to thrive."

"So what do we do about it?" Gray asked.

"There are several eradication and mitigation practices being carried out across the United States," Finn answered. "National parks, local agriculture and forestry departments, conservation groups, and so on. One popular method is to bring in predators from the plant's native area, like, say, a beetle that's adept at eating the leaves of the plant to negate invasive growth.

"*We* here at the Sentry, however," Finn stated, grabbing one bundle of toadflax and a pot, "do what we can by gently uprooting them in the field and relocating them, either to places where they can be contained and used for medicinal purposes, or back to their native area of the world." Using one hand, Finn made a well in the soil of the terracotta pot, then gently placed the toadflax in, root-first.

"Those roots don't look so bad," Gabby remarked.

"Ah," Finn chuckled, "that is because yesterday morning, the plant master herself, Ms. Jules Moreau, came with me to the field and used her powers to recede their root systems. This made it easy for us to remove them from the soil and separate them into individual plants, suitable for potting and transport." Finn flashed their wide, enthusiastic smile at Jules.

Ellie watched Jules's cheeks turn a vibrant shade of fuchsia. It nearly matched the petals on one of the stalks of hollyhocks.

"So! Today we will pot these," Finn instructed, gesturing to the pots on the tables. "We'll be keeping a few, sending some others to some herbalists for medicinal purposes, some to other Sentry branches for research. The rest will go to a greenhouse in India, where it is a native plant. If you can, strengthen the roots a bit in the soil before taking each completed pot to the shelves on the south wall." They gestured to shelves outfitted with UV lights. "If you do not have that ability, please drop your finished pot with Jules."

And with that, they all went to work. Ellie slid a pot toward her and dug into its soil with her fingertips. The feeling instantly calmed her. She'd always loved the tactile sensation of shoving her hands into dirt or mud or clay or sand.

She placed her toadflax into the pot like she was handling a sleeping kitten or a tiny baby bird and gently covered the roots with soil. She felt the roots' relief at being tucked back into the earth. Latching on to their energy, she closed her eyes and tried to imagine strengthening them . . . *growing* them. She opened her eyes and saw the plant wriggle the tiniest bit, its leaves twitching as though a slight breeze swept through the room. She could even hear the roots stretch and lengthen, though how she *heard* that, she had no idea.

"Seems like a happy toadflax!" Finn remarked, standing behind Ellie's left shoulder. "So, what's your first impression of Mountain Harbor?"

"It's great! Although I have to admit, this might be my favorite part," Ellie said, looking around the Greenhouse. "Although that could change whenever I get to see some animals."

Finn smiled. "Yes, this area is pretty impressive. Not to mention important. We try to grow a majority of our food here. Everything here is as sustainable as we can make it! Right down to the solar panels at the helicopter pad."

"Helicopter?" Parker sputtered in awe.

"Yes!" Finn chuckled. "Two, actually. And they run on sustainable biofuel. A special blend of plants and used cooking oil."

"Whoa..." Parker breathed. It seemed she had found something even more exciting than uniforms.

"Whoa is right," Finn replied. "If anyone had told twelve-year-old me I'd be flying a helicopter to and from a hidden base in an old mine, I wouldn't have believed them. Sometimes I still can't believe it! When I say it out loud, it always sounds like I'm some kind of superspy."

Ellie knew that was exactly what her sister was thinking.

"Where is your twin?" Ellie asked, hoping it wasn't too nosy.

"She didn't want to join," Finn answered, shrugging lightly. "When we were about your age, we trained with our father, then spent a few summers here. But she was always really interested in a future that didn't involve this life. When we graduated high school, the Sentry asked us to return as full-time members, but she had already been accepted to Columbia's pre-law program. She always felt her way of helping was to become a lawyer. While I always knew I needed to get my hands dirty." They held their hands up, wiggling their slender, soil-marked fingers.

"You don't wear a bracelet," Parker remarked.

Finn shrugged again. "It doesn't do much for me anymore. The bracelet is sort of a connector—a conductor between you and your twin's energies—so that if you're apart, you can still feel that special bond and balance that fuels our powers. But if your twin stops using their powers, then you don't have anything to connect to."

Ellie knew exactly what Finn was talking about. Her powers felt different without the bracelet—fuzzier, murkier, overcast. It was like a radio that could only emit static. Once she slipped the bracelet on, she could tune the radio to an actual station she could make sense out of, and when Parker was right next to her, it amplified the frequency, like the crystal-clear sound from a fancy speaker system.

"Is that what happened with Aiden's twin?" Ellie asked, hoping she wasn't overstepping. "They didn't want to join?"

She looked up toward the other potting table, watching Aiden throw his head back and laugh as he joked with Jules and Len. She tried to imagine what Aiden's twin must be like but came up short. It was too hard to imagine another person with those gray eyes.

"No," Finn said, their tone turning somber. "I'm afraid Aiden lost his twin brother in a tragic accident. When he was young."

"Oh." A stab of sympathy pierced Ellie's chest, knowing exactly how it must have felt for Aiden to lose such an important person.

"He doesn't like to talk about it," Finn continued. "Without his twin, his powers are diminished, but he definitely still has some. And he wants to help! The director isn't really in the habit of turning anyone away, with numbers being so low. Twin or no twin, the Sentry needs everyone we can get!"

"Why are there so few members?" Ellie said.

Finn shrugged. "I wish I could figure it out. Best I can guess is people don't care about helping the world anymore. But then I sound like a cynical adult." They let out a tiny laugh, then sighed. "What I *want* to believe is what my sister tells me when I ask her why she didn't join. She just felt like her powers weren't her *true power*. Like this wasn't the path that was meant for her, and she could bring about more change if she followed her calling. Now, if you'll excuse me, I think I need to gently remind Gabby for the tenth time this summer that flowers don't like to be *pinched*, even if it looks like you're making them talk." Finn smiled and took off toward Gabby at the opposite end of the table.

"That's sad about Aiden's twin," Parker whispered.

"Yeah," Ellie nodded. "When he was giving us the tour, I thought I picked up on a sadness from him. It wasn't like anything I'd felt before."

"Can you do the root thing?" Parker asked Ellie.

"I think so, yeah," Ellie replied.

"Cool," Parker said, sliding two completed pots toward her. "Because that is not my specialty."

Ellie put her hands on the side of Parker's first pot and closed her eyes, gathering her focus. But her concentration was immediately shattered by the sound of an explosion.

She shot her eyes open to see a dark shadow slide over the Greenhouse as a cloud covered the entirety of the glass wall, blocking out the afternoon sun. Ellie let go of the pot and backed away from the table in confusion.

SMASH! A pane of greenhouse glass broke into a thousand pieces, cascading like crystal rain onto the stone floor.

Immediately, *something* started coming in through the broken window—a slick, inky tendril. One massive black arm, then another, coiled into the space, dancing and slithering like an eel. Whatever it was looked like a cross between a cloud and a giant squid—both smoky and solid, heavy and light, able to reach and stretch and float wherever it wished.

"The Danger!" Jules yelled, as another pane of glass rained down from above.

CHAPTER SIX

As the terrifying tendrils crept closer and closer, Parker shrank from the potting table, retreating until her back hit the cold stone wall. Her breath came in jagged gasps as her heartbeat pounded in her ears. She knew the Danger was always lurking, but she'd believed Sadie's promise that Mountain Harbor was safe. Now, only hours into their time here, Parker felt caught off guard—unable to act, never mind process exactly what was happening.

Luckily, everyone else seemed to instinctively mobilize. Someone—Parker couldn't tell who—used their powers to send the shards of broken glass hurtling back at the Danger like daggers. But the cloud of black smoke absorbed the glass without seeming bothered at all.

"I've got this!" Jules announced with a confident, self-assured grin. She leapt over the potting table and positioned herself between the terrifying mass and the rest of them.

Parker watched as vines from a nearby plant thickened and widened to monstrous size in a matter of seconds, spreading across the room like massive green snakes. Within moments, they were wrapping around the black tendrils, growing stronger, squeezing and constricting. It was like watching an arm wrestling match from another dimension, as the two warring tentacles struggled against one another. Jules looked focused with all her might as she succeeded in pushing the inky arms back toward the glass wall. But a minute later, they came hurtling back into the space.

"It's too strong!" Jules called at last.

Ellie darted over to her. Parker couldn't believe that she was still glued to the wall in fear as usually cautious Ellie jumped into the fray without a moment's hesitation.

"I have an idea!" Ellie shouted.

"I can help!" yelled Casey, as he ran to her side.

Ellie held up her hands like a wizard as the snaking green vines suddenly grew vicious, fang-like thorns. Casey faced his palms at the Danger and pushed, like he was moving a heavy piece of furniture, causing a swirl of white to form inside the black cloud.

"Great idea! Freeze it out, Case!" cheered Finn. "Len! Gabby! Jump in!"

Len and Gabby jumped to action, scrambling to Casey's side.

A hair-raising shriek pierced the air. It was a sharp, high-pitched metallic whine that sounded to Parker like a thousand people had just dragged their forks across their plates in unison. The disgusting black tentacles shuddered, at last retreating from the barbed green vines and slithering out of the Greenhouse the way they'd come in.

Casey's snow cloud grew and grew, whirling with the intensity of a tornado and unleashing impressively sized chunks of snow and ice. A full-blown blizzard raged inside the Danger's oppressive veil of smoke, until suddenly the blizzard appeared to overtake it, breaking it down into thin wisps.

As the winter vortex dissolved the black smoke, Parker noticed there was something at its center—a solid sphere. It was a dark orb, inky black and shiny, almost like onyx. At first, it appeared to be floating, suspended in the Danger's vortex. But as she held her focus on it, she saw it wasn't inert like the gem it resembled. No, whatever it was seemed to be almost alive. Parker watched as it twisted and churned, changing shape along its edges, constricting and expanding in a regular rhythm.

It *beat* like a *heart*.

With another shriek like grating metal, the smoke cloud completely dissipated. As the last bits of smoke cleared, the solid black heart retreated, seemingly absorbed into the ether. Within moments, the sun returned, its light shimmering on the snow that now surrounded them.

Everyone in the room gathered in a huddle, cheering and patting each other on the back.

"Once again, the Danger doesn't hold a flame to the Sentry!" Jules whooped triumphantly. She squeezed Ellie's shoulder. "Nice work with the thorns, new kid."

"Thanks," Ellie said, looking gratified.

Parker wanted to join in, if only to congratulate her sister on her clever move, but she stayed rooted in place. She felt safer with her spine, her two palms, touching the solid stone. Because something about that room didn't feel completely safe just yet. She couldn't put her finger on it. Maybe, she thought, it was the frigid cold from the manifested blizzard, which still lingered in the air. Maybe it was just residual fear still coursing through her bloodstream. Or maybe . . .

She started to speak, but her voice came out strangled and squeaky, disappearing into the din of the group celebration.

"What is it, Parker?" Finn asked, appearing at her side. Apparently, they had heard her.

"I don't—I don't think it's gone," she muttered. "I feel, I mean, it's still—"

Before she could get the words out, a thunderous roar erupted. It was easily the loudest sound Parker had ever heard. It shattered the remaining panes of glass and caused the earth to quake beneath their feet. Before anyone could make sense of what had happened, the Danger descended upon them like a hurricane, whipping glass and rubble through the air, turning the sky black, stealing the breath right from Parker's chest.

She heard shouting, but the wind was so loud she couldn't make out any words. Finn ducked to avoid being hit by flying debris. Pots, plants, leaves, and soil flew across the room. The other students cowered, fighting against the gale-force gusts that were strong enough to topple them to the ground. Parker watched as Aiden knocked a potting table on its side and gestured for the others to come crouch behind it.

Parker had to do something.

The tentacles swung back into the room, thrashing around with frantic vengeance, smashing everything in their path. Another blizzard cloud formed, but the Danger sucked it in like a light snack, consuming it whole.

Then, from somewhere deep within the shouting, Parker heard something else. Her fingertips pulsed as the stone wall hummed beneath them. Suddenly, her whole body seemed to reverberate with energy—a familiar but foreign energy.

She whipped around and examined the wall, running her palms across the large, smooth slab of granite fused into the stony surface. She felt its energy. What's more, she *heard* its voice. And though she couldn't make out words in any recognizable language, she knew what it was saying: *Something inside me is* special. *Something inside me is* powerful. *You can use that power. Channel it through you and let me help.*

Electricity crackled at the tips of her fingers, funneling into her from the surface of the rock. The longer she touched it, the more her power continued to fork and vein and spread until it formed what felt to Parker like a huge electrical net. Instinctively, she pulled more energy from the slab. With an echoing CRACK, the granite ripped away from the cave wall. For a split second, Parker filled with panic, thinking that the entire wall might topple over onto her, but she quickly realized she was in complete control of it.

She guided the granite slab away from the wall, backing up to give it space. It groaned as its heavy bottom edge dragged along the stone floor. With surprising ease, she lifted the rock up over her head. She wasn't sure exactly what to do with the massive stone, but it kept whispering to her, telling her how to use its hidden power. And now it was telling her it wanted to fly. Using all the energy she could muster, she sent the slab hurtling toward the Danger, right at its beating heart–like center.

The rock soared above the others' heads, bound for the menacing cloud. It felt to Parker like the whole thing happened in slow motion. When it finally made contact with the Danger's inner core, the stone ruptured, splitting in two with a deafening crack. A beam of white light erupted from the granite, bathing the room in brightness. Parker had to shield her eyes against the flash. The two granite pieces clattered to the ground, where they instantly crumbled into dust.

The Danger screamed—at least, that's the only way Parker could think to describe the sound that echoed through her head—as the bright white light vanished as quickly as it had appeared. The Danger's heart began to shudder. In an explosion of embers, the once-beating orb ruptured, and with a final howl of defeat, the Danger vanished.

Now, Parker sensed, the room was finally safe.

She took a moment to catch her breath and center herself. But as soon as she looked up, she realized everyone was staring at her. She felt her cheeks flush at the attention.

Finn stepped close and stood in front of her.

"How did you do that?" they asked.

"I—I didn't do it," Parker answered. "The rock did it."

"The rock did it?" Finn echoed.

"It told me it had power inside of it," she explained, "so I just, I don't know, I guess I listened."

Moreau and Sadie came barreling into the disheveled Greenhouse.

"What in the world happened here?" Moreau uttered, surveying the room with wide eyes. Even from behind her thick glasses, the shock was palpable.

"The Danger," Len and Jules answered in unison.

"What?" Sadie gasped in shock. "It's here?"

"Is everyone okay?" Moreau asked, snapping back to fearless leader mode.

"Some bruised knees and egos, I'd guess," Finn answered. "But otherwise safe."

"Well, I'd like to get everyone looked over, just in case," Moreau declared. "I expect each of you to check in with me or Ms. Powers before dinner, is that understood?"

A chorus of mumbled affirmations sounded in response.

"Finn," Moreau said, turning to Finn, her eyes twitching over Parker with a look of suspicion as she did, "my office. Now. I need a full report."

"Of course, Director Moreau," Finn said, and the two exited the Greenhouse.

Sadie locked eyes with Parker. *Thank goodness*, Parker thought. She needed someone to help her make sense of whatever the heck had just happened. She didn't know whether to be scared, confused, proud, excited, or maybe all of them at once. But Sadie turned on her heel and followed the other adults out of the Greenhouse. Parker felt deflated.

Wearily, the others pulled themselves to their feet.

"Thrilling," Len groaned. "We successfully fend off the Danger and now my mom is going to drag it out by playing nurse all afternoon. Honestly, I don't know why she's making such a big deal out of this."

"Because it's a huge freaking deal!" Jules snapped.

"We fight the Danger all the time," Len argued.

"Out there!" Jules said, waving her arms toward the broken glass wall. "It never comes *here*! This is freakishly abnormal." At that, Jules squinted in the direction of Parker and Ellie.

Parker couldn't read people as well as rocks, but she was getting the distinct impression that Jules wasn't her biggest fan.

"Whatever," Len sighed in exasperation. "Go visit Mom, then."

Everyone trudged out of the Greenhouse, their exhaustion obvious in every step. Everyone except for Parker, that is, whose ears were still humming and buzzing with adrenaline. Ellie grabbed her hand.

"What was that all about?" she asked.

Parker shrugged. "I heard the rock," Parker said. "Just like you hear animals—I *heard* the rock."

"No, I mean, what is with the Danger attacking literally the minute we start our training?" Ellie questioned.

Parker stopped walking and turned to Ellie. "You think it's here because of us?"

"I don't know what to think," Ellie replied. "But I think it's an awfully big coincidence that we showed up today and so did the Danger."

Ellie headed through the hallway toward the bunks. Parker watched for a moment, unable to will her own feet to follow. She felt like someone had just dumped a bucket of ice water over her.

Parker had been more excited about Mountain Harbor than pretty much anything ever. From the moment Sadie appeared at their door, she'd felt this pull she could only describe as *fate*, like she was on her way to becoming exactly who she was meant to be. Sure, she got excited about uniforms and spy lingo, and occasionally, cute boys with shaggy blond hair. But what really mattered was the mission—to train, and grow, and then do whatever was necessary to save their mother.

She couldn't wait until the moment they were reunited, when her mom saw how much the twins had grown up. And she couldn't wait to show her that even though they'd missed her terribly, she and Ellie had pulled through. Against all odds, they had made it work, just like her.

Really the only thing Parker wanted more than to see her mom again was for her mother to feel proud of the person she'd become. Until this moment, she had never doubted it would come to pass. The thought that the Danger could destroy that chilled Parker to her core.

CHAPTER SEVEN

Back in Harborville, Ellie had grown used to waking up to her sister's jarring alarm as the bright daylight flooded their sunny bedroom. At Haven, she'd gotten accustomed to the loudmouthed rooster who screamed before the sun had even begun its crawl above the horizon. So the gentle, soothing melody piping over the Mountain Harbor audio system wasn't exactly going to do it for her. In fact, after the exhausting day of travel, orientation, and fighting off the Danger, all that the gentle nudge served to do was make her go right back to sleep. She yanked the cool sheets up over her head, covering it entirely, and closed her eyes tight.

Arlo groaned at the foot of the bed.

What's with the spa music? He echoed her thoughts exactly. *Don't they know we got up before dawn yesterday?*

"I'm sure they don't care," Ellie muttered into her pillow.

If they actually wanted to get us up, they should have brought us breakfast.

"Who are you talking to?" Parker asked from the top bunk,

her voice sounding chipper and not the slightest bit groggy. "Oh, right. Silly question. Morning, Arlo."

Tell her to be quiet, came his response.

"He says good morning," Ellie groaned, her eyes still shut tightly. Parker hopped off the top bunk and turned the lights on.

Liar! I said no such thing. Tell her to turn those lights off. And then to go get me breakfast. If she insists on being awake, might as well make herself useful.

Ellie sighed. Arlo complaining in her head was about as soothing as Parker's impossible chipperness.

"I saw a calendar in the dining room yesterday," Parker announced. Ellie pulled the sheet down with one finger, just enough to spy her sister standing in front of the mirror, vigorously brushing her long brown hair. "It said today's breakfast is pancake buffet. Let's get down there before all the good stuff is gone!"

Now we're talking, Arlo perked up.

"I'm fine with plain pancakes," Ellie replied through a yawn that used just about every muscle in her face. "Breakfast goes until eight-thirty. Jules told me that yesterday."

"Jules," Parker repeated the name, clicking her tongue.

"What's wrong with Jules?" Ellie mumbled.

"Nothing, she's just . . ." Parker trailed off. Ellie suspected she couldn't find the right word because there wasn't anything actually wrong with Jules and Parker was just jealous of her. "I get a weird feeling there."

"You don't like her because you want to be her," Ellie remarked, rubbing her eyes to rid them of crusty sleep. "You like being the *captain* of the team. You like being in charge. But Jules is, like, nineteen and has way more experience."

"No, that's not it." Parker shook her head. She pulled her hair back into a sleek ponytail and secured it with an elastic. "Or, I don't know, maybe that's it." She whipped around and pointed a finger at Ellie. "But don't go being best buds with her because of your little 'killer plant' routine yesterday, okay? We need to make sure we can trust her first."

"Listen to you, sounding all paranoid. I thought you were the one with no worries about coming here." Ellie could practically feel Parker's suspicion radiating from across the room.

"Look, you just never know," Parker said with a shrug as she readied her toothbrush at the sink. She started brushing, talking through the foaming, frothing paste. Ellie was used to this form of Parker's communication and understood every word. "I just get this weird sense like she's not happy we're here. Almost like she was glad when the Danger first showed up, because she thought she'd be able to show off." She brushed more and more aggressively as she spoke. "I know it doesn't make sense. But I think we'd be smart to keep our distance." A dribble of bubbly paste hit the floor with a light *splat*.

Ellie shrugged and rummaged through her bag for something to wear to breakfast, since uniforms weren't required until the first training session. She wished Sadie had mentioned the whole uniform thing—she wouldn't have packed so much. She unearthed a wrinkly shirt, followed by an equally rumpled pair of jeans before finally deciding she might as well go ahead and unpack.

Ellie dumped the contents onto the bed, sifting through the pile for her favorite yellow hoodie. She found it with no issue, but something else was curiously missing—the compass she'd stashed in the front pocket.

Don't panic, she told herself, reasoning it could have shifted around at any point while they were traveling. One by one, she held up every piece of clothing she'd packed, shaking them out, checking the pockets, hoping the compass might suddenly appear.

"What are you doing?" Parker asked.

Ellie sighed. "I can't find the compass. I know put it in the pocket of my yellow hoodie, which I put at the bottom of my bag, for safekeeping. But now it doesn't seem to be anywhere."

Parker looked stricken. "Are you absolutely certain you packed it?"

"Yes," Ellie nodded. "I'm positive. It's the very first thing I packed."

"Where could it be?" Parker started to pace. "Do you think someone could have taken it? But we never let the bags out of our sight."

"Yesterday!" Ellie gasped. "When Aiden was giving us the tour. We left our stuff in the Atrium." Hot panic washed over her. It was awful enough that their mother's gift had gone missing but truly unsettling to think it might have been stolen.

"Jules!" Parker hissed. "I bet she took it."

"All right, let's not jump to conclusions."

The sound of footsteps and muffled voices echoed through the door as the other trainees made their way to breakfast.

"Let's go get breakfast," Parker said, snapping into what Ellie recognized as her patented hyperdrive mode. "We can scope out the others and see if anyone looks guilty. And while we're at it, we might as well eat."

Ellie just nodded, afraid that if she spoke, she might start to cry. She couldn't believe the compass was gone. She should have been more careful. She should have kept it on her at every moment. She should have never let it out of her sight. It was more than just a missing item; it felt like she had let her mother down.

"It's not your fault," Parker said, prompting a look of surprise from Ellie. "What? Just because I can't read your thoughts doesn't mean I don't know how you think." And with that, she grabbed Ellie's hand and led her out of the room.

Bring me back a pancake! Arlo called after them. *Or three. Or seven?*

But they were moving so fast that Ellie barely heard him.

No sooner had they made up their pancake stacks—Ellie's with blueberries, banana, and chocolate chips, and Parker's with sprinkles, whipped cream, and strawberries—than Jules made a beeline for the buffet table and tapped Ellie on the shoulder.

Ellie gasped, then immediately hoped Jules couldn't read her suspicion.

"Sorry to startle you. When you're done eating," Jules spoke softly, but just loud enough for everyone at the nearby table to overhear if they were interested, "my mother would like to see you in her office."

Well, Ellie thought, *if they weren't listening before, they definitely are now.*

"What is this about?" Parker snapped.

"I don't know," Jules replied with an innocent shake of her head. "She doesn't talk to me about confidential things, like reviewing other trainees' *records*."

She said the word *records* at least three decibels louder than was necessary. Parker went red in the face, and Ellie got the distinct feeling that, even if they weren't in trouble, Jules wanted everyone to think they were.

"She probably just wants your help fixing up the Greenhouse," Aiden remarked, giving Parker a fist bump as he headed for a second trip down the buffet. "I bet you could have it rebuilt in no time. First Ellie at the train tracks, now Parker's magic boulder. Is there anything these two can't tackle?"

Jules glared at Aiden, then stomped back to her own table, where she dropped into her chair with a thud.

Maybe Parker was right, Ellie thought, vowing to keep one eye on Jules until they had a better sense of things. It reminded her of something they always said in Parker's spy movies—keep your friends close and your enemies closer.

The pancakes didn't quite settle in Ellie's stomach. Her panic over the missing compass, coupled with the worry over whether or not they were in trouble—on their first full day, no less—was wreaking havoc on her gut. And now, the sight of Director Moreau certainly wasn't helping.

Ellie sat in a stiff wooden chair stationed across from the director's massive timber plank desk. The chair's thick wooden arms were carved to resemble some sort of creature—a griffin, maybe—stretching from face to tail. It was the first piece of furniture Ellie had ever encountered that looked like it was actively roaring at her. To her left, Parker sat in a matching seat, her leg bouncing wildly.

"There's no need to worry, ladies," Moreau said, clearly picking up on the tension. Her voice sounded soothing and a bit amused. "This isn't the principal's office or anything."

"We're not in trouble?" Parker asked.

"Goodness, no!" Moreau laughed a melodious laugh, like a fancy set of wind chimes. "What on earth would you be in trouble for?"

Parker shrugged.

That question is a trap, Ellie heard Parker's thoughts. *She wants us to admit something!*

Ellie piped up. "We're still so new, we weren't sure if . . . if there were certain powers we weren't allowed to use, or something. We're still learning the rules."

"Oh, girls!" Moreau laughed. "It sounds like you've read too many books about magic schools. But this isn't a school, it's a training program. And you're not in trouble for anything, yesterday or otherwise. In fact, quite the opposite."

Ellie exhaled. Until that moment, she hadn't even noticed she'd been holding her breath.

Moreau continued, "From what I heard, you two saved the Greenhouse and, frankly, everyone in it. I'm beyond thankful and, I must admit, also profoundly impressed."

I wish Mom could hear this, Parker thought. Ellie gave a tiny nod in agreement.

"Now, I don't want you to take this praise, or what I'm going to say next, to mean you're done with your training—you're *not*," Moreau explained, her hands tented in front of her. "However, I do believe that you are talented and capable enough to start going out on missions."

At the mention of her favorite word, Parker began tapping her foot so excitedly Ellie thought it might wear a hole through the floor. Ellie wished she felt the same level of excitement over *missions*. But she worried it was just an impressive sounding word for running right after the Danger.

"Usually," Moreau continued, "we require a minimum of two summer-long training sessions and one hundred hours of Mountain Harbor fieldwork logged before we approve trainees for official Sentry missions..." Moreau trailed off and sighed deeply. "Oh, who am I kidding? Listen, I know I was rather prickly with your aunt yesterday, but the fact of the matter is, our numbers are declining. Rapidly. When you two showed up—after everything I had just heard about you from my sister, Barbara—I was honestly ecstatic. And though I don't want to admit it, and you're not going to tell her I said this, I'm glad your aunt is here too."

"Jules said that yesterday was the first time the Danger attacked the base itself," Ellie said. "Do you think..."

She couldn't finish her thought, but she knew she didn't need to.

"Do I think the Danger was after you two, specifically?" Moreau finished. "I'd be lying if I said the thought *hadn't* crossed my mind. Field encounters with the Danger have been increasing over the past several months, but, as Juliette mentioned, we haven't had an attack on the base for over a decade. Since your mother was here."

Ellie and Parker exchanged a nervous glance.

"Honestly, though, it's neither my concern nor my duty to assess *why* the Danger does what it does," Moreau explained. "Many have tried, and the general consensus has always been that the Danger is a supernatural embodiment of pure chaos. My duty is to do my best to prepare Sentry members to face and conquer the Danger, wherever they may encounter it."

Like when they're out on missions, Ellie added silently.

"Parker, I'd specifically like to find some time to work with you on your imprint abilities," Moreau continued.

"Imprint abilities?" Parker echoed. "What's that?"

"Finn told me that you could feel the energy left in the boulder by the last person who'd manipulated it, is that correct?" Moreau asked.

"Yeah, I guess so. When I touched the rock, I just kind of heard it talking."

"We refer to that energy as an 'imprint'," Moreau explained. "Not many Sentry members have the ability to sense those imprints, let alone manipulate them to their advantage as you did. It is a highly coveted skill among our ranks—one that I also possess and have spent much time and effort cultivating. As soon as you get back, I'd love to assess your current skill level and see how I might help hone your abilities."

Parker smiled. "That sounds great," she said.

"What do you mean 'as soon as we get back'?" Ellie asked.

"Oh, I guess I forgot to mention that!" Moreau laughed. "Your first mission is today."

Ellie and Parker shared another glance.

Parker had never looked so proud, including that one time at the Ultimate regional championship when she caught a pass in the defense's end zone to score the winning point and the entire school had cheered. Ellie, on the other hand, felt like she might lose her pancakes all over the big wooden desk. *What would this mission entail? Was it smart to leave base when there was a thief in their midst? What if that person decided to strike again? What if the director was in on it, and that's why she was sending them away?* It felt like nowhere was safe.

"You have twenty minutes to get in uniform and meet Instructor DeSoto at the helicopter pad," Moreau said, as though this were a perfectly normal sentence to utter before lunch. "And pack a canteen. You're headed to the desert."

CHAPTER EIGHT

Parker had never been on a helicopter before and frankly she couldn't wait. As she strode to the helicopter pad wearing her official Sentry uniform, bound for her first Sentry mission, she thought how the only thing that could possibly make it any cooler was an aviation headset worn at a high altitude.

But her excitement quickly gave way to nerves when she saw who would be joining them—Gabby and *Gray*. Moreau hadn't mentioned anything about that. Parker smoothed her uniform and ran her palms over her hair. She hoped she wouldn't seem hopelessly inexperienced. She hoped the headset wouldn't look dorky. She hoped she wouldn't get airsick. She suddenly regretted that third pancake.

"Calm down," Ellie whispered. "We're supposed to be on alert about the Danger, remember? Who cares about some boy?"

As Parker watched Gray's sandy hair blowing in the breeze, she was loath to admit that *she* cared.

The Van Loon twins appeared to be engaged in intense conversation but stopped speaking the moment they saw they had company.

"Oh," Gabby said, making no effort to hide her annoyance. "I had no idea you two would be joining us."

What was with these people? Parker wondered. First Jules, and now this? Talk about a welcoming bunch.

"Gabby!" Gray growled at her. Then he smiled at the girls. "What my sister means to say is 'Hi! Glad you two are joining us,'" he said.

"Not what I meant to say at all, actually," Gabby muttered, tossing her blond braid over her shoulder.

"We didn't know we were coming either," Ellie said with a shrug. "Sorry if it messes something up for you guys."

"Do *not* apologize, Ellie," Gray said. "It doesn't ruin anything. The more the merrier! We're glad you're here. At least, I am."

Parker giggled, maybe a bit too enthusiastically. Thankfully, Finn hopped out of the helicopter and brought her laughter to a stop.

"All systems are go!" they said, then gestured to the helicopter. "You McFaddens ever been on a chopper before?"

Ellie shook her head. "No, we haven't."

"I think you're gonna dig it," Finn said. "And if you don't, well, the ride is short! Everyone in. Safety belts on! Hands and feet inside the chopper at all times—yada yada yada, you know the drill."

They all climbed in, took their seats, strapped in, and put on the headphones as the blades spun faster and faster. And then they were off.

The ride was short and thankfully without drama. Gray and Gabby didn't say a word to one another, or to anyone, for the entire trip. Ellie gripped the seat with white knuckles, as though she was on a roller coaster that might take a dive at any moment, but she made it through just fine. Parker did her best to enjoy the moment—the sky, the landscape, the feeling of *flying*—but it all went by in a blur.

A few minutes later, the five of them stood in the oppressive sun, their boots crunching in the dry, sandy dirt. Parker scanned the horizon in every direction. This wasn't like any desert she'd seen in movies. No wavy lines, no bright golden sand, not even a mirage. This was merely a field of dusty dirt, littered with big rocks and sad bushes that looked like they were missing half their foliage.

Finn knelt down and examined the dusty earth, propping their impressively sized sunglasses on top of their head to get a better look.

"Here," they said, pointing at a spot in the dirt in front of them. There was seemingly nothing special about it, just a random dirt spot located between two sparkling rocks that were roughly the size of backpacks.

Parker stepped closer and squinted. Barely discernible in the layer of dusty earth, something—some sort of current—was moving through the dirt. It looked like a brush stroke swished from one rock to the other. Then, farther along, there came another swish, arcing the opposite way.

"What is that?" Ellie asked.

"It looks like an invisible snake," Parker added.

Finn looked up at her and smirked. "Something like that." They stood and brushed the dust from their knees. "All right. Everyone keep their eyes peeled. Not much wind today, so we should be able to track this thing pretty easily." Finn pulled their phone from one of the zillion cargo pockets lining their khaki shorts and started blasting old school rock 'n' roll.

"Won't that scare it?" Gray asked.

"It might, if it were a snake," Finn answered with a mischievous smile. "For now, your job is to track it."

Parker led the tracking, no matter how hard she tried to let the others catch up or even pass her. The next brushstroke, the next swish just seemed to jump out to her—*call* to her. When she'd look back at Finn to make sure she was on the right track, they just smiled at her with apparent amusement, sometimes offering a thumbs-up.

After about twenty minutes, Parker noticed something on the horizon. From where she stood, she couldn't tell exactly what it was. It just looked like a sandy blur, moving back and forth. She glanced back at Finn with apprehension.

"Ah, there it is," Finn said.

"But what *is* it?" Gabby asked.

"Let's get closer and you tell me," Finn suggested.

They tramped across the dry earth with Parker leading the pack, until finally she was close enough to see that the mysterious blur looked like it was swirling. Like a whirlpool or a tiny tornado. It stood only about two feet tall, like something constructed by a toddler. The closer she got, the less it appeared to be made of sand and the more it seemed to be made of smoke.

She swallowed. There was no good reason for smoke to appear in the desert. Unless . . . And that's when she saw them—a dozen or so little tendrils, spaghetti thin and black as a starless midnight, swishing back and forth in the dirt-colored sand.

Gray and Ellie finally caught up to her, flanking her on either side. Ellie gasped as Gray sputtered. "It's a—a—it's a baby Danger?"

Finn stepped right up to the miniature monstrosity. "Precisely."

"Wait a minute," Gabby chimed in as she arrived, panting.

"You brought *four* of us here, to this hundred-degree dust-bowl, to see a baby Danger?"

Finn clucked their tongue at Gabby's attitude. "Well, Miss Van Loon," they said wryly, "before I brought you to this hundred-degree dustbowl, did you know where the Danger came from?"

She opened her mouth, but only a dejected squeak came out.

Gray raised his hand.

"Yes, Gray," Finn said. They kicked some dirt into the Danger's vortex, which visibly slowed its movement.

"Are you saying the Danger originates here?" Gray asked. "And why do we call it 'the' Danger if there are actually a lot of them? Or are they all part of one entity?"

"Fantastic questions, Gray!" Finn exclaimed. "And that's exactly why I brought you all here. Because the short answer is, we still don't know."

"And the long answer?" Gray asked.

"What we do know is that the Danger is, uh, are electrical atmospheric anomalies." Finn smiled. "The point is, we're still trying to understand what it is. Barbara Boudin pioneered the current research on the origins and patterns of the Danger, using sophisticated weather tracking technology. I worked with Ms. Boudin for three years on researching and tracking these *Fountainheads*, as she called them."

"Where does the research currently stand?" Ellie asked.

Finn sighed. "You mostly know the story. Dwindling enrollment numbers. Increased Danger and climate change activity. Director Moreau was never completely supportive of her sister's area of study, so when Barb was needed elsewhere, that's where she went."

"Haven," Parker muttered.

"Yes." Finn nodded. "Along with several other missions."

"So, did you guys figure out what causes these atmospheric electrical whatevers?" Gray asked.

Parker usually liked to be the one asking questions, but in this one instance, she found she didn't mind one bit when Gray was the one speaking.

"Electrical atmospheric anomalies," Finn corrected. "And sort of. They seem to be linked to what the Sentry has long referred to as 'areas of imbalance.' Places where the natural balance is just out of whack. I'll show you what I mean once we bag this little guy."

Finn kicked another round of dirt at the Fountainhead.

"Why do you keep kicking sand on it?" Gabby asked.

"Ah! This brings us to our Geology lesson. What is sand made up of?"

"This area seems to be primarily composed of a silica base," said Gray, drawing a line in the dirt with his toe.

"And what's this?" Finn interjected, pulling something from their oversize knapsack. It looked like a box, but instead of the typical wood or cardboard, it was made of shiny, polished crystal.

"Quartz," Parker answered, not realizing she had blurted out the answer until the word was out of her mouth.

"Yes! In our studies of the Fountainheads, Boudin and I found that the Danger is particularly vulnerable to certain materials—specific minerals, chemicals, and so on. One of those minerals is *quartz*."

"That's probably why Parker's granite bomb worked so well in the Greenhouse!" Gray exclaimed. "Granite contains quartz!"

"I do think that's part of it," Finn said, smiling at Parker. "I also think that particular slab of granite was full of a certain energy, something even more powerful than quartz. But that's an excellent inference, Gray.

"And, to answer the first part of Gabby's question," they continued, "the reason we are here today is that even if Director Moreau doesn't yet recognize the value of her sister's research, she definitely recognizes the value of stopping these little guys while it's easy, before they turn into the big ones."

With a confidence that Parker could only imagine came from having done this dozens of times, Finn unlatched the top of the quartz box and brought it closer to the Danger. The creature let out a high-pitched whine as it began to shrink in size. When it was small enough to fit inside the container,

Finn lowered the box and slammed it shut over the tiny swirling Fountainhead. It was swift and sharp, like a mousetrap in a cartoon.

"Wait," Gabby groaned, as Finn latched the box shut, "you're not bringing that thing back with us, are you?"

Finn looked at Gabby, as though deciding whether to answer. Instead, they announced "And now, it's time for the second part of our lesson."

The next part of the lesson turned out to be in the local town. Parker wasn't sure what she expected from a tiny desert community, miles from the nearest city or body of water—one little main street of Southwestern adobe buildings, surrounded by an assortment of cacti? Instead, she saw lawn after lawn of lush green grass. As the glossy suburb continued for block after block, she couldn't believe her eyes. There were shrubs and bushes and flowering gardens. There was a sprawling park and a shopping center, complete with a massive fountain. At one point, Parker bent down to touch the grass to check if it was fake, and found it was very, very real.

"Oh yeah. It's real. There's a new golf course on the other side of town too," Finn remarked, shrugging and raising their brows. "Real grass, everywhere. Watered twice a day, every day!"

"Creating an area of imbalance?" Parker questioned.

"You know it," Finn said. "The more environmental imbalances we create, the more electric atmospheric anomalies appear."

"Don't they *know* this isn't sustainable?" Ellie asked. "Don't they get that grass doesn't belong in the desert? That this isn't how it's supposed to be?"

"Oh," Finn sighed in exasperation. "If they do, they don't care. Humans like to think we have control over the natural world, that we can shape it to look and feel and *be* the way we want it to. Weed killer, bug killer, lawns in the desert, fake snow at ski resorts. At first, it's just about our yards. Then it's burning down the Amazon to make room for more cattle. But people have a hard time seeing the big picture. They don't worry about things like drought and the declining bee population because they're too focused on their own little corner."

Finn stopped to survey the trainees. Four faces, each sullener than the next.

"All right, enough of this talk for now. Let's all take a breather—grab a snack, explore the town, and meet me back here in twenty."

Finn headed toward a cafe, then stopped and turned back to the group. "This place has the best cinnamon lattes this side of the Colorado River, but if you're not into coffee, there are some cool gift shops and a bookstore too."

Parker scanned the line of stores and saw one that caught her eye. It looked quaint and a little quirky, full of Southwestern charm, the way she'd expected the whole town to be.

"I'm going to grab a smoothie," Gabby said, breaking off from the group. Parker was not sad to see her go. She headed in the direction of the little shop, with Ellie and Gray close behind.

The Sonora Trade Post smelled like sage, old leather books, and also, for some reason, coconut. Inside the shop, which seemed dark compared to the bright desert sun, Parker saw a wall full of taffy bins and a display of various specialty sweets—rock candy, oversize rainbow lollipops, boxes of fudge. So that's why it smelled sweet.

While Ellie maneuvered to the candy section, Parker was immediately drawn to a display of rocks and crystals. Baskets of loose stones, polished and raw, lined the shelves, and bracelets and necklaces hung from hooks on the wall above. Her hand instinctively reached out toward a necklace—a simple cord with a jagged chunk of a milky, pale pink crystal.

"Rose quartz," Gray said, appearing at her side. Parker already knew what it was. That was basic knowledge for someone considering a possible future career as a museum curator. "Good idea, Parker," he added.

Parker hadn't even thought about what Finn had just said about the Danger's vulnerability to quartz—she just thought the necklace was pretty. But now she supposed it could be useful too.

Gray grabbed a bracelet of polished smoky quartz. "We can be quartz buddies," he said with a grin, sliding the bracelet on his wrist and holding it up to show her.

"You seem to know a bunch about rocks, huh?" Parker asked him. "Like when you knew the sand was made of silica."

"Yeah, that kinda stuff comes up a bunch in my research," he said.

"Research about what?" Parker asked.

"About the recent surge in Danger activity," he answered. "The diminishing effect of our powers against it. The presence of anomalies. That kind of thing."

"Anomalies?"

"Yeah," Gray answered, his eyes lighting up at the chance to share his findings. "The Sentry archives say that back in the day, when anomalies were present, it created the same kind of surge in Danger activity that we've been experiencing lately."

"And what is an anomaly?" Parker asked, feeling nervous to hear the response.

"Oh! That's what we call a twinless person with powers," Gray said.

"Like, when someone's twin isn't around?" She thought of Aunt Sadie and Finn and Aiden, whose counterparts were no longer around. Even Moreau and Boudin were working at a distance.

Gray leaned in like he was about to tell Parker a secret. "Well, about a hundred years ago, at a Sentry branch called Crystal Lake, the first documented anomaly was born. They came into the world without a twin but had the power of two people—the full range of abilities that would normally be split between twins."

"So there's only been one anomaly?" Ellie asked, rapt. Parker had been so enthralled in the story she hadn't realized her sister had joined them.

"No. Legend has it there were others. But the documentation isn't great."

Parker clutched the crystal necklace as a chill ran up her arms.

"Anyway," Gray said, "maybe you could join me in the library sometime and we can do some more digging. I first got interested in the topic because, as you probably noticed, my twin and I don't always see eye to eye. I don't know if we're cut out to work together forever, but I love the Sentry and I don't want to give up my powers before I have to." A furrow creased his handsome forehead. "Anyway, we should probably pay for this stuff and get going before Finn comes looking for us."

"Did we want to get any candy while we're here?" Parker asked.

"Done and done," said Ellie, holding up a massive bag of assorted taffy. *Who would ever want to be an anomaly*, Parker thought, *when you could have a twin who could read your mind?*

Just as Finn had promised, they were back at Mountain Harbor by lunch. Parker and Ellie even had a few minutes to stash their candy and change into fresh uniforms.

In the mess hall, Jules and Aiden were already assembling their salads when the group from the mission walked in.

"Where were you all this morning?" Aiden questioned as he took a seat with his tray.

"Quick trip to the desert," Finn answered. "The McFaddens were a last-minute addition."

Parker was typically never one to get excited about a salad, but she was so hungry from the mission that she couldn't wait to put some leaves on a plate.

Jules looked up at her from the other side of the salad bar cart.

"Oh, hey, Parker," she said with a smile. (A fake smile if ever Parker had seen one.) "My mom says you need to meet her in her office, *again*, as soon as you're done with lunch."

It took every ounce of control in Parker's body to keep from lobbing a cherry tomato at Jules. Why did she have to make these little announcements in front of EVERYONE?

Parker knew exactly why—it was how bullies asserted their dominance. She had watched enough animal documentaries AND high school rom-coms to know that.

"Wow, twice in one day?" Gabby sneered, loading a plate with baby carrots. "That might be a new record."

Parker chose to ignore that line as she spoke directly to Jules. "I'm sure it's because of our special one-on-one training."

Jules slammed the salad tongs back into the trough of lettuce, causing tiny bits of roughage to fly every which way.

"*What* did you say?"

"I guess I have some special talent," Parker said with a nonchalant shrug. "And it's very rare. But luckily, the director has it too."

Jules's eyes narrowed as her cheeks turned a deep shade of crimson. Parker felt a twinge of remorse but quickly reminded herself that Jules had spent their last two encounters trying to embarrass her in front of everyone. And besides, Parker was just telling her the truth.

"Nice, Parker!" Aiden called through a mouthful of lettuce. He was a remarkably sloppy eater, Parker thought, noting the lettuce scraps dotting the table around him. "I can't wait to hear more about your special talent. If it has anything to do with splitting that giant rock, I'm sure it's awesome."

Parker and Ellie took a spot slightly removed from the others and ate their salads in silence, content to stay out of the fray.

For the rest of lunch, Gray and Gabby debated the historical inaccuracies of the movie *Anastasia*. Jules and Len spoke in hushed tones, probably plotting how to ruin Parker's life. Aiden continued to eat with the grace of a rabbit in a hutch.

As soon as she was finished, Parker excused herself, cleared her dishes, and grabbed an oatmeal raisin cookie the size of her hand. She slipped out of the mess hall, eating the cookie as she headed to her lesson with Moreau.

Alone in the cavernous halls, winding her way toward the office, Parker grew focused on the echoes of her boots on the stone floor and the way the sounds of her breath seemed to fill all the air around her. She became so transfixed that she ran directly into Aunt Sadie outside Moreau's door.

"There you are! How are you? How was your first mission?" she asked.

"I'm fine," Parker said. She hoped she sounded convincing.

"Really?" Sadie asked, cocking her head. "I'm sorry I couldn't check in on you both last night. I know you've had quite the time here so far. But it's all part of gaining the experience for the larger mission at hand—rescuing your mother."

"Maybe we don't actually need all this training," Parker sputtered. "Maybe we're ready to save her *now*."

Sadie smiled, stroking a soft hand across the top of Parker's head. The movement seemed unpracticed at first—like when a person who is *not* a dog person attempts to pet a random dog on the sidewalk—but after a moment, Sadie seemed to gain confidence and pulled Parker into a tentative hug.

"Soon," she said, her voice quiet but firm. "Can you trust that I have a plan? And that you do need a bit more experience? I promise, there is a right time and that time is not now."

Parker let out a breath she hadn't even realized she'd been holding. She nodded and let her fists unfurl.

"Thank you," Sadie murmured. "I know you don't have much reason to trust me. I'm practically a stranger to you. But it means a lot to me that you do."

"You don't feel like a stranger," Parker said. She felt an unfamiliar longing for more of Sadie's motherly touch on her head. It had been so long since she'd been hugged or touched by her own mother. It felt like "soon" could never come fast enough.

Sadie squeezed her shoulder. "Have a good training with Director Moreau. It will get us much closer to being able to rescue Ginny. I have a job to finish, but I'll see you tomorrow."

Like clockwork, as if she'd been waiting specifically for Sadie to make her exit, Moreau popped her head out of her office and trained her glistening hawk eyes on Parker.

"Are you ready? It's time."

CHAPTER NINE

It was after dinner and the Atrium was empty, other than Ellie and Parker. Even Arlo, who had been curled up by the fireplace, had wandered off to go "exploring"—dog slang for finding a snack.

"Your turn," Parker said, gesturing to the Carcassonne set up on the coffee table between them.

Ellie squinted at the game as the fire crackled and snapped behind her. She found it hard to concentrate with this jazz music—Parker's choice—blaring on the stereo. Parker said her basketball coach had always played it for ball handling drills because the rhythm was perfect for dribbling. But Ellie found it a bit too chaotic for doing much of anything.

Carcassonne was a strategic world-building game where you used your tiles to construct things like roads and castles. So far, though, Parker was on the verge of finishing a massive twenty-two-point castle while Ellie could barely extend her dinky little road.

Before Ellie had a chance to find a spot for her less-than-satisfactory tile, several sets of footsteps echoed from the corridor leading to the Atrium. She turned to see Aiden, Jules, and Len saunter in and scan the room for seats. Len threw herself onto the loveseat nearest Ellie, sprawling across it so that her nearly six-foot frame filled it from arm to arm.

"HOW can you stand this? Turn it off!" she groaned, swatting at the air around her face.

"The music?" Ellie asked, secretly pleased to have an ally.

"No," Len sighed. "That stupid fire!"

Jules produced a remote from a small end table and ended the fire with one click.

"You know, you could have done that yourself," she said to her sister. "Without a remote."

"Yes, well, I'm tired," Len growled. "So I'd rather conserve my energy for the next imminent disaster."

Jules squeezed onto the tiny bit of loveseat next to sister, while Aiden pulled over a small, upholstered chair and took a seat.

"Do you think there'll be another attack?" Aiden said, crossing his legs. His long limbs looked especially endless next to the small chair, giving him the appearance of a spider.

"Don't you?" said Len.

"I don't know. I guess I'm hoping what happened in the Greenhouse was an anomaly," Aiden said.

"Well, something certainly feels weird to *me*," Jules said, looking pointedly in the direction of the McFaddens. "So I'm staying on high alert."

"We probably shouldn't alarm the new recruits," Aiden said. "Although it seems like they're probably the ones who'll wind up protecting all of us."

"We certainly could've used them on our mission today," Len snorted.

Ellie had heard about it—Len had spent the afternoon fighting a wildfire in Montana along with Casey and Cassie Phillips. They'd all come back looking exhausted, covered in scratches, bruises, and soot.

"It was bad?" Parker asked.

"The worst," Len answered.

"What happened?" Parker pressed. "Did the Danger show up?"

"Might as well have." Len sighed, shaking her head. "It felt just like what happened in the Greenhouse. Every time we'd make headway against the fire, it would come roaring back."

"Well, was it the Danger or not?" Aiden asked.

"I'm not sure. It was almost like the fire *was* the Danger, you know?" Len mused. "But Ms. Powers said it was just the result of dry brush."

"Ms. Powers—wait—*Sadie* went with you?" Parker sputtered. "That's weird."

Since when did their aunt go on missions?

"I know!" Len suddenly sitting up. "I don't even understand why she went with us. I'm a senior Sentry member! I'm almost twenty years old! I don't need training, never mind a babysitter."

"You know exactly why Mom sent her, Len," Jules rebutted.

"If you're going to bring up that—that stupid Painted Desert thing again . . . it was an *accident*," Len rebutted. "Just a dumb mistake. It wasn't my power fading, no matter what Mom thinks, or says."

"Len, it's okay if it was," Aiden said, taking on the gentle tone of a counselor. "It happens to everyone at some point. We all lose our powers in adulthood. But it doesn't mean you don't still have value, or that you can't still help." Aiden shrugged.

"Yeah, well," Len grumbled, "it's *not* happening to me, so let's just drop it." She pulled her knees up to her chest, hugging her arms around them. "And that's not what happened today anyway," she added, defensively. "If you ask me, Sadie made it worse."

"What do you mean?" Ellie asked. "Like, she did something *wrong*?"

Len shrugged and shook her head. "No, it just . . . It felt different. It felt—I don't know—out of balance, or something."

A chill tingled down Ellie's spine. Maybe the apprehension she'd been feeling about this place wasn't just her nerves. Maybe the Danger showing up right when they arrived wasn't a coincidence. And maybe it had nothing to do with her and Parker.

Maybe it was *Sadie*.

The rest of the evening was spent playing Carcassonne, without any further discussion of official Sentry business. Two hours and two games later, the group was in much better spirits. Everyone, that is, except for Ellie.

When they headed back to their bunk, Ellie watched her sister pick out pajamas, humming the melody to one of the K-pop songs that Len had just played and loudly sung all the words to. She could tell Parker was in a good mood, but that didn't make it any easier to figure out how to say what she needed to. Parker wouldn't like it, Ellie knew that. And all the delicate phrasing in the world wasn't going to change that. So she decided to just say it.

"Parker," Ellie started, "I've been thinking."

"Is this about me helping you with that hundred-gallon saltwater aquarium you want? Because if so, I think I'm ready for it," Parker said.

"Really?" Ellie replied, caught off guard. She had asked for a saltwater aquarium the previous spring, right before their eleventh birthday, and their dad had said both of them would have to commit to the responsibility. Parker had just discovered Ultimate Frisbee and wasn't interested in committing to feeding clown fish or testing pH. So instead, Ellie had gotten her fish, Walter, who could survive alone in freshwater under only her care.

"No, that's not it, but good to know!" Ellie said, "It's actually about all the stuff going on around here. Since we got here, I mean."

Parker plopped down on the bottom bunk next to her and pulled her hair out of its ponytail. "What a mess, huh? All this Danger stuff."

"Such a mess," Ellie agreed, nodding. "But, listen. I think, um, I mean I have a feeling that, uh, maybe it has something to do with Sadie."

Parker's eyes narrowed and her lips puckered. She stared at Ellie in silence for a full thirty seconds before slowly asking, "What do you mean?"

"Think about it," Ellie said. "Last night, we were worried that the Danger had something to do with *us* coming here. That it was too much of a coincidence for it to *not* be about us. But *we* weren't the only ones who got here yesterday. So did Sadie."

"Ellie—"

"And remember what Director Moreau said in her office this morning?" Ellie plowed on. "The last time the Danger attacked Mountain Harbor itself was back when our mom was here. That means Sadie would have been here too!"

"She also said that the Danger is chaos and not to waste time trying to assign meaning to it," Parker pointed out.

"And do you actually believe that after everything Finn taught us today?" Ellie rebutted.

Parker shook her head. "No, I don't. But I don't believe that this has anything to do with Sadie either."

"You heard what Len said tonight, Parker," Ellie pressed. "Sadie went with them to fight the wildfire and it all went sideways."

"She also sounded pretty defensive about her powers fading too," Parker argued. "We have no way of knowing what really happened. We should talk to Sadie and get her side of the story before we take anything those Moreau twins say as fact."

"And you think Sadie will tell the truth?" Ellie asked.

"Yes," Parker said, matter-of-factly. "I do. Why don't you trust her, Ellie? She's family!"

"She may be family, but she's basically a stranger," Ellie said. "Mom never even told us about her. And look what happened the last time we trusted Mom's family!"

"Sadie isn't Mabel," Parker growled.

"I'm not necessarily saying she's doing anything on purpose, Parker," Ellie said. "She might not even know she's causing anything. But Len said Sadie made things feel 'out of balance.' What if Sadie is creating and attracting chaos because her energy is out of whack without her twin, or something?"

Parker seemed to ponder the idea. "Yes, that's what it is!" she shouted, with a declarative finger in the air.

"It is?" Ellie echoed, shocked that Parker came around so quickly.

"Yes! There's an imbalance." Parker said. "But it's not Sadie."

Ellie sighed. *So much for Parker coming around*, she thought.

"But somebody here *is* out of whack, likely because their twin is gone. Or missing. Or dead, or nonexistent—we're not sure yet."

"We? Who's we?"

"Gray mentioned that thing in the gift shop," Parker explained. "The anomalies. People with powers who don't have a twin. They—the twinless power-wielders—make the Danger worse. Gray wants me to help him do more research in the library archives. You should come with us."

"Okay," Ellie said slowly. "I think that's a good idea. But what if Sadie *is* the anomaly?"

"Why do you want Sadie to be the problem, Ellie?" Parker snapped.

"I don't!" Ellie defended. "I just don't want us putting our trust in someone who's going to hurt us! Again!"

Parker sighed and shook her head. "You just want to be right about something because I was right about Mom this whole time."

"What? No—Parker, it has nothing to do with that—"

"I'm done talking about this Sadie stuff," Parker said, scrambling up the ladder to the top bunk and burrowing under the covers. "If you want to keep being suspicious of the person who wants to help us save our mother, fine. But don't expect me to join you."

Ellie flopped back on her bed and sighed.

Are you two done bickering? Arlo's voice sounded as he crawled out from his hiding spot under the bed.

"Hi, Arlo," she murmured, as he hopped onto the blanket next to her. "What have you been up to?"

Oh, you know, just being a dog. Sniffing around, doing dog stuff, trying to stay out of family drama. He curled into a perfect circle at her side, like a poppy seed bagel. *Uh, so I might have eaten some of that taffy earlier. It was a mistake! Okay fine, it wasn't. But it was so good. It tasted like bananas I think.*

"You thief!" Ellie hissed, petting his head. "You need to be careful, or you'll get a stomachache."

Nah, I'm fine. How could something that tasty possibly be bad for me?

He was asleep within moments, snoring softly in Ellie's direction with decidedly banana-scented breath. Ellie, on the other hand, didn't expect to sleep for a while. She wondered if she was right about Sadie, and if it had been worth bringing up at all. But there was no way of knowing. They would need to wait and see.

CHAPTER TEN

Parker tried to fall asleep. She really did. But as Arlo snored and Ellie tossed and turned on the bunk beneath her, Parker felt certain she would burst into flames at any moment under the suffocating comforter. The previous night, she'd had no trouble falling asleep. But now her anger had turned the temperature up.

She kicked the comforter completely off the top bunk, but that wasn't enough to cool her down. It wasn't really the blanket's fault and she knew that. Parker ran hot, especially when she was ticked off—and she was extremely ticked off about Ellie's accusations regarding Sadie.

Slipping out of bed, she sighed in relief when her feet hit the cool stone ground. She especially loved how the floor made no noise underfoot, unlike the squeaks and groans of the hundred-year-old hardwood back home in Harborville. Parker had never once successfully snuck down the hall for a snack or a round of computer Solitaire without waking her dad.

Arlo rolled over on his side and let out a groan. For a medium-sized dog, his sleep sounds were the stuff of a much larger animal—a bear, perhaps, or a gorilla. Parker worried that perhaps she had woken him, but once his snoring resumed, she figured the coast was clear. She grabbed her sneakers, opened the door just enough to slip through, and closed it gently behind her.

Parker padded down the hallway, which was dark save for the few dim lights hanging every few feet. Her stomach grumbled the way it always did whenever she found herself awake past midnight. Once anger and hunger joined forces, she would have no chance of falling asleep, so she headed to the mess hall to see what might be available for snacking.

As she passed through the mosaic hallway, she noticed a gentle hum that she hadn't picked up on before. It was soft but urgent, like a forest full of cicadas or the sounds of a far-off choir. Was it the twinkle lights, giving off some sort of electrical noise? Was it just the normal sound of being underground, and she hadn't been able to hear it until it was otherwise completely silent?

No, she realized, pausing. The humming came from *imprints*, the imprints within every stone that composed the mosaic. She thought back to her earlier lesson with Director Moreau. Sometimes, an energy was strong enough to *hear*, like she had with the granite slab. But sometimes, Moreau had said, you have to "establish a connection."

Well, she figured, there was no harm in practicing. Parker knelt down and touched her finger to one of the ruby-red crystals that made up the image of flowers vining up the column.

I will protect you, the red crystal hummed at her. Parker yanked her fingers back as an icy cold shiver ran up her arms. Because she knew that voice. It was unmistakable.

The voice was Sadie's.

After her momentary shock that she was able to pick out *actual people's* imprints—a skill that Director Moreau said would take months of training to acquire and years to master—she wondered what to do with this information. Part of her wanted to rush back and tell Ellie, as if it were proof of Sadie's innocence. But instead, she simply sighed, stood up, and continued toward the mess hall. If Ellie had made up her mind to distrust Sadie, that was her own problem, and there probably wasn't much Parker could do to convince her otherwise. Once Parker and Ellie found themselves on opposite sides of something, they tended to stay there out of stubbornness. Parker wasn't sure if that was a Powers thing or a Taurus thing. Or both.

It didn't matter anyway. Just like Parker couldn't hear animals or intuit thoughts and feelings like Ellie could, Ellie couldn't hear the imprints, so it would just be Parker's word against hers.

Parker's footsteps echoed through the empty mess hall as she pulled open the door to the walk-in cooler and let the frigid air swallow her. Her body shivered as her skin prickled into gooseflesh, but it felt *amazing* compared to the stifling heat of her comforter. She took a few deep breaths, enjoying both the cold and the silence, then grabbed a raspberry yogurt and headed to the pantry for some granola.

As she ate, she wandered slowly around the mess hall, checking out the tea selection, discovering a cupboard filled with cake pans and cookie cutters, and finally pausing to read everything on the bulletin board. After scanning the menu calendar for the rest of the month—make-your-own pizza on Friday nights and crepe brunch on Sundays—she noticed another sheet of paper also formatted like a calendar. The title read *July Midnight Patrol*. Well, that was news. She didn't know they had *any* patrol here, midnight or otherwise.

Her eyes swept over the calendar, relieved to discover that neither her name, nor Ellie's, was listed on any of the time slots. But after a moment, she began to feel miffed at the omission. Why *weren't* she and Ellie on the list? Moreau had said she was promoting them—giving them missions and more responsibility. So, why wouldn't they be trusted with the same tasks as everyone else?

Her eyes zeroed in on the fine print text at the bottom of the page.

Sentries: Please report for duty at the director's office before pro-
ceeding to the Tower. Patrol begins at 10p and ends at 4a. Patrollers
are excused from the following morning's lesson/exercise.

What was the Tower? This was the first she'd heard of it. That hadn't been a stop on Aiden's welcome tour. Thankfully, the bulletin board also held a map of Mountain Harbor, showing that the Tower sat in the very center of it all. It was labeled as having the highest elevation, which, Parker reasoned, must mean it sat at the very top of the mountain—near the boulder field where they had first entered the base.

"At least somebody drew a map of this place," Parker grumbled to herself, remembering the cryptic directions and confusing hidden passages she'd endured just to search for a book to read at Haven House.

Tapping her finger on that day's square on the patrol calendar, Parker saw that Aiden and Jules were on patrol duty. She pulled the map off the bulletin board and folded it until it fit in the pocket of her flannel pajama pants. She could go back to bed, she reasoned, and be subject to Arlo's snoring. Or she could go in search of answers. The choice was clear.

The midnight mountain air was almost chilly enough to make Parker run back to her comforter. Overhead, she saw hundreds of stars—more than she'd ever known were in the sky—glistening against the black of night. The rumble of low voices and crunching footsteps reminded her why she'd come, and it wasn't to stargaze. In the distance, she could just make out two silhouettes standing at the tree line. They were taller than her—the size of adults—one longer and lankier than the other. Aiden and Jules. Parker headed in their direction, stepping carefully on the uneven terrain.

"Parker?" Aiden called. "What are you doing up here?"

"What are you doing up at all?" Jules added.

"Couldn't sleep," she said, with a shrug.

"Ah," Aiden said, flashing that perfect smile. "Whenever I can't sleep, a snack always seems to help."

"I had a snack," Parker interrupted. "That's when I saw the patrol schedule. And wondered why my name isn't on it."

Even in the dim moonlight, Parker could see Aiden and Jules exchange a *look*.

"It's a new program," Jules explained.

"The director just started it yesterday," Aiden added. "Because of the Greenhouse attack. We figured it can't hurt to have eyes on the situation at all times."

"Wait—you're not on the schedule at all?" Jules clarified. "Ever? Like the whole month?"

"Nope," Parker replied. "Ellie neither."

"Well, that's dumb," Jules huffed, crossing her arms. "If I have to stay up all night staring at nothing, you should too."

"The director probably just didn't want to overwhelm you," Aiden said. "Given your special training and all. Speaking of which, how is that going?"

Parker shrugged. "Pretty good, I guess."

"What are you and my mom working on?" Jules pressed, stepping in closer.

"Well, right now I'm learning to work with imprints. She'll hand me a bunch of different objects—like rocks and teacups and stuff—and have me, I don't know, listen to them and report what I hear."

"Listen to teacups?" Aiden said.

"Yeah," Parker said with a nod.

"Well, do they say anything?" he asked.

"Not the teacups," Parker answered. "Not that I could hear, anyway."

"Listening to ceramicware?" Jules scoffed. "What kind of skill is that? Are talking teacups supposed to save us? This isn't *Beauty and the Beast*."

"Ignore her, Parker," Aiden said. "She's just jealous."

"What?!" Jules spat. "I'm not jealous of a twelve-year-old!"

"No, you're jealous of a person who has the same ability as your mom and gets to take private lessons from her," he said. "We all are, to be honest."

"Why?" Parker asked bluntly.

"All the good stuff is ahead of you," he said. "You're just

learning how to harness your powers, and over the coming years they'll only grow stronger. Once you reach adulthood, for most people, your powers start to diminish. For Jules and me, if we want to stay in the Sentry well into our adulthood, we'll have to take on supervisor or administrative roles. But our best missions are probably behind us."

"Speak for yourself," Jules grumbled. "My powers are just fine, thanks."

"Anyway, I think it's safe to say you're the most powerful one here right now!" Aiden gave Parker a fist bump, which only made her feel embarrassed.

Jules crossed her arms.

"Oh, c'mon, Jules," Aiden said. "You're nineteen years old and out here without your twin. You're finally on *my* level!"

"Cut it out, Baxter," Jules growled. "I don't know how many times I have to say this, but my powers haven't faded one bit."

"Whatever you say, Future Director Moreau," Aiden said, bowing dramatically in front of her, like she was royalty.

Jules laughed and smacked his upper arm. "Stop it. You know it's going to be Director Powers if Sadie has her way. And then probably Director Van Loon, and then Director McFadden!"

"Me?!" Parker asked, pointing at her own face.

"Yeah, you," Jules said in a begrudging tone. "You saved the whole base on your first day here, you have your superspecial rare ability, your mom is a Sentry legend . . . need I go on?"

Parker blushed, thankful that at least this time, in the dark, no one else could see.

"So, yeah," Jules conceded, her voice soft, "maybe I'm a little bit jealous. But it's not your fault."

Parker smiled. "For what it's worth, my sister says I'm jealous of you too."

"Oh yeah? And why is that? Because my mom's in charge? Or because I'm rude to new kids and act superior despite the part where my powers are rapidly disappearing?"

"No, because you're like the captain of the team," Parker fangirled. "You're so confident. You know things. People look up to you. Powers or no powers, you're all the things I want to be."

Jules grabbed Parker's shoulder and gave it a comforting squeeze. "You will be, Parker. You're already on your way."

Parker smiled. Maybe she'd been wrong about Jules after all.

"I think you two should hug it out," Aiden said, breaking the silence.

"Oh, Aiden." Jules laughed.

"No, I'm serious," he said. "I think we've made some major progress here today. Same time next week?" They all laughed as Aiden's expression suddenly turned serious. "As heartwarming as this little exchange has been, I think it's probably time for us to change lookout points."

The three turned in unison to head to the southern edge of the tree line, where Aiden had indicated they should patrol next. As Parker made her way through the flowery meadow, she swore she saw a *snowflake* twirling around in front of her face. She stopped for a moment, squinting into the dark.

It's July, she thought. Surely it couldn't have been snow. She knew they sometimes saw snow in the Rockies in May or even early June, but *July*? It was probably just dust, she decided.

"Parker, you don't have to stay out here with us," Aiden called over his shoulder, as he marched farther ahead. "You should go rest. I'm sure Finn has a big day planned for tomorrow."

She supposed he was right. No sooner had she opened her mouth to reply than she saw another snowflake, twinkling like glitter in the moonlight. Then another. Then a dozen more. Within moments, the air was dotted with glistening flakes, falling in a steady stream.

"What the heck?" she heard Jules utter. "Are you guys seeing this?!"

"Of course I'm seeing it, Jules," Aiden said. "We should get inside before we freeze!"

"No, Aiden," Jules snapped back. "This is exactly why we're out here. We need to sound the alarm!"

"Over some snow?" Aiden argued. "It's *weather*, Jules. We're in the mountains. You want to wake everyone up to make snow angels?"

"This isn't normal. I've lived here for seven years, and I've never seen anything like this—" As Jules carried on, Parker held out her hand and let the snowflakes melt against her skin. She shuddered and recoiled as they melted into smudges of thick, black ash. Parker had never lived in the mountains before, but even she knew that snow melting into inky smog *definitely* wasn't normal.

"She's right!" Parker called out to them. "Sound the alarm!"

"Why are you two being so dramatic?" Aiden groaned in exasperation. "It's just snow!"

"No, it's not," Parker declared, sprinting toward them and holding out her ink-dotted hand. "It's the Danger."

CHAPTER ELEVEN

Arlo jumped to all fours and barked wildly, jarring Ellie awake. She'd been lost inside a dream about a berry farm run by a family of hedgehogs—equal parts adorable and delicious. She pushed sweaty locks of hair out of her face and squinted at Arlo in the dark.

"What's up?" she croaked.

Danger danger! Arlo turned in a circle.

"Like, *the* Danger?"

Something feels wrong! Something feels off!

Ellie sat up, but before she could climb out of bed, the lights came on and an alarm started wailing.

"What the heck?" She realized no one had shared the protocol for fire safety or routine evacuations, never mind earsplitting alarms in the middle of the night.

"Parker?" she called, reaching up to wake her sister on the top bunk. She was greeted with a tangle of empty sheets. Parker was gone.

Ellie flew into panic mode, scrambling to the door and out into the hallway. Casey and Cassie rushed toward her, Casey still pulling on his uniform shirt and Cassie yanking her hair into a topknot as they ran.

"What's going on?" Ellie called.

"Get dressed and get to the Atrium," Cassie said. Ellie was surprised at how calm she seemed. "An overnight alarm only sounds for one of two reasons. Natural disaster or the Danger."

"I'm guessing it's not a natural disaster," Ellie groaned.

"No," Cassie sighed, "probably not. See you up there."

She took off in a sprint down the corridor. Ellie ducked back into her room to change into her uniform.

"Where is Parker?" she wondered aloud.

Arlo whined. *Knowing your sister, probably right in the middle of the action!*

Ellie's heart flipped. She changed into her uniform at lightning speed, pulled her boots on, and ran out the door. She made it to the end of the corridor and was almost to the stairs when she nearly slammed into a uniformed body. Someone was standing as still as a statue, seemingly unaware of the chaos unfolding around them.

"Sadie?" Ellie asked. "Is everything okay?"

Sadie turned, her eyes never leaving the phone in her hand. She looked like she had seen a ghost.

"I have to go," she said, matter-of-factly.

"Right now? What's happening?"

Her aunt held up her phone. *Come ASAP*, read the message. Ellie glanced at the top of the screen to see who'd sent it. *Ginny*.

"Wait, what?" Ellie entertained what felt like a million competing thoughts. "Is she in immediate danger? Can we come with you? And are you saying we could have been texting or calling her this entire time?!"

"No," Sadie replied. "She doesn't have reception. She only comes up for emergencies."

"Only comes *up*? So this is an emergency?"

"Yes, and I don't have time to explain," Sadie said, turning and rushing up the stairs.

"Wait! If you're going, then I'm going," Ellie declared. "And Parker is coming too."

"Michelle is never going to let you leave, Ellie," Sadie said. "Especially not right now. You need to stay and help hold down the fort."

"You brought us here to save our mom!" Ellie yelled. She was surprised at her own volume.

"And you will," Sadie said. "But right now, I have to go. Let me figure out what's going on, and I'll reach out as soon as I have a plan."

"But what if something happens to you?" The words caught in Ellie's throat.

Sadie whipped around, her expression softer than Ellie had ever seen it.

"Oh, sweetheart," she murmured, brushing Ellie's stray hairs from her forehead. "Something is always going to be happening. But I'm going to do my best not to let it happen to our family anymore."

A sob broke from Ellie's throat as Sadie clutched her to her chest, squeezing her in the tightest hug Ellie could ever remember receiving.

"I need you to trust me, okay? I know it isn't easy. But I promise I'll reach out as soon as I can." Ellie just nodded as Sadie took off running, her backpack bouncing with the force of her steps.

As confusing as it was, there was no time to waste. Ellie continued in the direction of the Atrium, afraid of what she might find. An icy cold breeze greeted her long before she got there, as the sound of howling wind drowned out the din of the alarm. But even that couldn't prepare her for the scene that greeted her. The Atrium was bathed in darkness, white snow blanketing every pane of glass. Most disturbing of all, no one was there.

"Hello?' Ellie called, dashing out of the Atrium and into the hall. She retraced her steps, running down the stairs and back toward the cabins, panicking more and more with every step. Where was everyone? Why was there no trace of them anywhere?

Outside! Arlo's voice rang out from inside the bunk. *I'm a working dog remember I'm useful and can smell things and I'm good at stuff why don't you let me help you!*

"Thanks, Arlo!" she called.

But I want to help!

"There you are!" Parker shouted. "We're all outside! Come on!"

"It's snowing?" Ellie asked.

"Full-on Danger blizzard," Parker answered with an emphatic nod. Ellie noticed she was wearing her pajamas and sneakers in place of her uniform. They sprinted down along the tree line, their feet crunching in the snow. Even though Ellie considered Parker to be capable of running basically nonstop, they were *both* completely winded by the time they saw the others.

"Parker! Ellie!" Finn waved their arms wildly, shouting over the howling wind. "We can't even find the Danger in these conditions! Parker, can you help Len and Gray clear a field of vision in the snow?" Parker nodded and dashed through the wall of dizzying white flurries without a moment's hesitation. "Ellie, I want you with Aiden and Gabby, due north. They're listening to the trees for any signs of contact with the Danger."

Ellie peered into the thick pine forest in front of her, where she could just make out two silhouettes about ten yards away. She trudged through the snow. It felt more like quicksand; her boots sank inches into the thick, crunchy drifts with every step. From behind her, Finn shouted, "Remember, as soon as you find the Danger, call it out!"

Aiden and Gabby looked like they were in deep concentration in the middle of the towering pines. Ellie didn't want to disrupt them, so she just copied what they were doing. Closing her eyes, she reached out and put her hand against the trunk of the nearest tree, as Gabby was doing.

She didn't hear anything. She didn't *feel* anything. But she knew what she was looking for. She remembered her time back at Haven when all those innocent animals had been brought there for healing—how scared they were, how much pain they were in. She had felt their pain and terror and heard the whispers of whatever had caused it. It was almost like the Danger left its own imprint, an embedded message of fear and harm.

Ellie opened her eyes and through the swirling snow could just make out Gabby nodding at her and pointing north. Ellie gave the thumbs up and moved in that direction.

For tree after tree, she heard nothing but complete calm, even amid the blizzard. Ellie was glad to discover these trees were so zen, though it didn't give her much information to work with. As she looked around, she realized she had lost the others. She no longer saw Gabby or Aiden. She couldn't see Finn and the meadow. She was deep in the trees to the north, where all she could hear were the winter gusts wailing in her ears. She reached out and grabbed on to the next tree trunk, mostly to keep herself steady as the wind attempted to knock her off her feet.

Immediately upon contact, her skin seared with pain. There it was.

Terror.

Her heart pounded as she let go of the tree and rushed to consult the next one. She closed her eyes as agony and panic filled her again, this time with more intensity.

Your fault, your fault!

Ellie breathed against the pain. She couldn't tell if the voice she was hearing in her head was the tree's ... or the Danger's.

You made your mother leave. You you you.

"What?" she uttered, pulling her hand away. "Who are you?" she shouted at the tree, feeling only slightly silly for expecting an answer. Hesitantly, she placed her fingertips back to the rough bark.

She didn't want you. She has a better life now. Give up.

Ellie yanked her hand away and roared at the top of her lungs. "North! North! Danger to the north!"

After a few moments, a crescendo of heavy footsteps headed toward her until she was surrounded by everyone from Mountain Harbor, including Director Moreau. The snow around them dissipated slightly, and Ellie saw the reason why: Parker, Len, and Casey held their arms up in the air, focusing their powers on controlling the storm.

And then they all saw it: writhing black tentacles winding around the tops of the pines, sucking the life out of them, turning their green needles to ash. The tentacles descended from a massive smog-cloud body that seemed almost to shimmer in the moonlit vortexes of snow and ice. It loomed over the Sentry, covering the entire forest, forming an inescapable dome of destruction.

Ellie had never seen anything so horrifying in her entire life.

"It wants to use snow?" Moreau shouted over the wind. "Well, then let's turn up the heat! Now!"

Flames erupted from Len's and Cassie's hands, spraying upward, past the snow and pines and into the Danger. A shriek echoed through the night, creating an eerie harmony with the howling blizzard wind. A bolt of lightning struck the Danger, nearly blinding Ellie with its flash. She regained her sight just in time to see the Danger's smoky orb of a body shudder as its tentacles whipped around in a confused frenzy.

"Yes, Casey!" Finn yelled. "Lightning is working! Aim for the core!"

Casey lifted his hands to the sky. This time, Parker did too. Two dazzling, forked bolts hit the Danger in unison. One of them must have struck the core, as the lightning frayed out and refracted, sending crackling offshoots in all directions.

"Everybody, down!" Moreau bellowed.

Ellie dove behind the trunk of a tree as a tongue of lightning sizzled in the snow where she had just stood. A loud crack and a scream pierced the air as Ellie whipped around to see a flaming pine tree hurtling toward the velvety white ground. Two figures were directly in its path.

CHAPTER TWELVE

Parker watched with dread as her bolt of lightning hit the Danger's core and branched out into dozens of dancing, scorching fingers. A loud crack echoed through the forest as the lightning hit one of the trees, splitting its trunk in two. As the tree turned into a tower of flame, it began to pitch to one side.

Jules and Aiden were directly beneath it.

"Juliette!" Moreau shrieked, as Aiden lunged forward, wrapping his body around Jules as though his slender frame could possibly shield her from the tree's impact.

Parker mustered every ounce of energy she had left and latched onto the nearest boulder, pulling it as quickly as she could toward what she hoped was the correct spot. At her urging, it slid easily across the ground, through the snow and mud. She had only a split second to doubt herself before she placed the boulder just below the tree's rapidly descending branches.

Charred needles and sparks rained down as the tree crashed into the rock, its descent halted just as Parker planned. She hoped that Aiden and Jules could get out from under the tree before the flames reached them.

"Jules?" Len called.

"Aiden?" yelled Finn, as a panicked Moreau bolted toward the fallen tree. But no sooner had she started in that direction when a slopping, gurgling whirlwind of mud and snow whipped up around them. It quickly extinguished the flames with a series of crackles, hisses, and spits. Smoke filled the air, rising in a great plume toward the sky, where the stars were almost visible again.

Aiden crawled out from beneath the charred branches, with Jules emerging right behind him. They were both caked with mud, their hair and faces covered in messy streaks.

"Who's responsible for this mud facial?" she asked.

Ellie sheepishly raised her hand.

"A McFadden," she laughed. "I should've known."

Aiden shook his head at her. "Of course you're laughing after we almost died."

"Well, as glad as I am that you're both alive and capable of laughter," Finn called, "the Danger is still out there."

"Are you sure?" Moreau asked them.

"The blizzard is still going."

But just as soon as Finn had made their declaration, the snow began to dissipate and within seconds had tapered off to nothing but a few stray flakes, fluttering through the air like the last remnants of confetti after New Year's Eve. Parker set her eyes on Finn's face, which had turned itself into a series of straight lines. Their lips were pressed tightly together, while their eyebrows looked like two dark brown shelves stationed beneath the faint, parallel lines spanning the width of their forehead.

"Is that . . . normal?" Parker asked.

Finn shook their head. "No," they answered. "It doesn't usually dissipate on cue. But it isn't normal for the Danger to attack us twice in the span of thirty-six hours either. Excuse me," they said, looking Parker in the eyes and shoving their hands in their coat pockets, "I need to make a phone call."

With that, they walked away, trudging across the muddied grounds and disappearing into the boulder field toward headquarters.

"I think we should all head back inside," Moreau announced. "Thankfully, the base seems to be untouched. Gray, Casey—can you keep watch out here for a bit longer? Just to be on the safe side."

The two boys nodded, and Moreau gently ushered Jules back toward the entrance.

"I'm fine, Mom," Jules groaned in embarrassment.

Ellie appeared at Parker's side. "Quick thinking with the boulder," she said.

They grinned at each other in the moonlight, and for a moment Parker felt settled, content with the role she had just played. But it lasted all of a second before Ellie's worried face brought her back to reality.

"We need to get back to the bunk," Ellie whispered. "There's something I need to tell you."

"Sadie's gone," Ellie said, as soon as she closed the bunk room door behind them. "She got this text from Mom, saying it was urgent and that she needed Sadie to go there immediately."

"I'm sorry, what? Mom can *text*?" Parker wrinkled her face in a mix of confusion and disbelief. "Why doesn't she text us?"

"I know, that's what I said. Sadie told me she doesn't usually have service. Something about how she has to *come up* in order to get it."

"Come up? From where? A submarine? A bunker?"

They began to change out of their wet, muddy clothes and into fresh pajamas, although upon hearing Ellie's latest update, Parker had to fight the urge to put on a clean uniform and go search for their mother herself. It was nearly two in the morning. It had been only a couple of hours since she'd gone searching for her late-night snack, but it felt like a million years had passed.

Ellie shrugged her shoulders up to her ears. "I don't know, but it seems weird to me that the whole reason we came to this camp—that was supposedly safe and is easily the most dangerous place I've been in my life—was so that we could help Sadie rescue Mom. And now she just ran off to do it without us!" She plunked herself down onto the bottom bunk and threw her hands up in confused exasperation. "Unless..." Ellie started to speak, then thought better of it.

"Unless what?"

"Unless Sadie isn't rescuing Mom at all."

Parker sat down on the bed next to Ellie. Arlo snuggled between the two of them with one ear perked up, listening intently.

"It is weird that she ran off without us," Parker sighed. "I agree. But I'm sure Sadie has her reasons, and she's probably not used to having to explain them to a couple of kids. Or who knows, maybe there's a good reason she didn't tell us more. Maybe there's someone here she doesn't trust and she doesn't want them knowing Mom's whereabouts. Maybe it was for our own protection."

"That just sounds like you're making excuses for her," Ellie stated.

"I'm not," Parker said. "I guess I'm just trying to see things from her point of view."

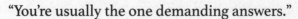

"You're usually the one demanding answers."

"I think I'm too tired to demand anything." Parker yawned.

"Sadie said she'd check in with us in the morning," Ellie said. "And let us know what was going on with Mom."

"Good. So we don't have long to wait. And until then, we can sleep," Parker declared, standing and making her way over to the ladder to the top bunk.

"Sleep! I don't know how you can think of sleep at a time like this," Ellie said, shaking her head in disbelief. "Aren't you worried? Aren't you afraid we'll miss something?"

Parker peered through the rungs of the ladder. "I hear you, but who knows what she's doing until she tells us? She could just be dropping off tacos or toilet paper for all we know." Ellie giggled below. "We might as well sleep so we have some energy tomorrow. What if we need to leave immediately to help with the rescue?"

Parker flung herself across the top bunk, her head landing perfectly on the cool pillow.

Ellie sighed. "You're right. And the sooner we go to sleep, the sooner we can wake up and have answers."

Parker heard Ellie's sheets rustle beneath her as the lamp clicked off. Within moments, she felt herself drifting off into the sort of heavy slumber that she couldn't find earlier. It felt like she was on a boat headed toward a night full of rest and dreams, and the river rapids were just carrying her toward it.

She didn't have to do anything at all. Just lie there and get closer and closer with every second, every breath . . .

"Parker?"

Parker's boat jerked off course, but she didn't open her eyes.

"Mm-hmm," she groaned in response.

"Have you ever . . . *heard* the Danger?" Ellie asked, tentatively. "Not just its howl, but its actual voice."

The boat rammed into the bank and Parker's eyes popped open. *So much for the peaceful night's rest*, she thought.

"Yes," she said slowly. "Why do you ask?"

"Well, that's what Finn had me doing out there. Listening to the trees to see if they had been touched by the Danger. But one time, I swear I heard the Danger instead of the tree."

Parker sat up slightly, propping herself on her elbow. "And what did it say?"

There was a moment of silence. When Ellie spoke, she sounded near tears. "It said it was my fault that Mom left."

"That's exactly what it said to me!" Parker said, remembering the sting of when she first heard those words in the forest outside Haven. Back then, the whole Danger thing made even less sense than it did now. But its message went straight to her core.

"Really?" Ellie whispered.

"Yes," Parker replied, as a mix of sadness and relief washed over her. As much as she hated to hear her sister feeling hurt, it was comforting to discover that someone else had heard it too.

"Do you think it's true?" Ellie spoke in a small voice. "Do you think that whatever happened to her had something to do with us?"

"When we were six years old?" Parker scoffed. "No way. What could we have done? We didn't know anything about any of this. We were just kids in first grade. I couldn't even read yet!"

"But why would it say that?"

"Um, because it's the Danger. Why would it attack out of nowhere with creepy tentacle-arms? Why would it do any of the weird stuff it does? You remember what Moreau said, right? You can't apply logic to its actions."

"I guess you're right," Ellie sighed.

"This is exactly what it wants," Parker said. "To make us feel bad, so we give up without a fight. But we're not going to do that, are we?"

Ellie didn't reply.

"Ellie?"

"No."

"No what?"

Ellie sighed. "No, we won't give up."

"Now, that's what I like to hear. Good night, Ellie. Good-night, Arlo."

Parker closed her eyes and within moments, she pushed her boat away from the shore.

The next morning, Parker's eyes were unwilling to open. She was normally one to pop out of bed like a jack-in-the-box, ready to greet the day. But now, her body would barely even move, let alone pop. Whatever amount of sleep she'd gotten, it hadn't been enough.

She groaned into her pillow, keeping her eyes tightly shut. *Technically*, she had been on midnight patrol with Aiden and Jules when the Danger came, so *technically,* Moreau should let her have the morning off from classes too.

"Parker," Ellie's voice drifted into her half-slumber, her words soft and barely audible. In her half-asleep state, Parker pictured a cartoon mouse that spoke with her sister's voice. "It's eight," the mouse said, "So I'm going to go eat. Want me to bring you back a breakfast burrito?"

Parker let out a loud grunt.

"I'll take that as a yes," the Ellie-mouse said, adding, "I still haven't heard anything from Sadie."

Parker heard the door slide open and closed.

Still haven't heard from Sadie . . .

Deep blues twisted in front of Parker, then shimmering aquas, then pale crystalline ceruleans. Water sloshed and splashed and filled her ears. *Don't breathe!* her brain shouted at her. *You're underwater! You can't—*

She breathed in. Nothing happened.

Okay, you can totally breathe water in this dream. Never mind! Carry on.

She sliced her arms through the water, expertly propelling herself forward like a mermaid. In what felt like moments—but really, what is time when you're in the middle of a dream state—her very efficient swimming had brought her to a submarine lodged in an underwater rock bed, surrounded by a rainbow assortment of fish and coral. She breathed, she swam, she blew bubbles, all effortlessly. She thought of Ellie's future saltwater tank. *Maybe I will bring her some of these fish,* she thought as she passed a school of tiny ones—hot pink and orange with bright purple tails, swishing and darting back and forth.

When she reached the submarine, she banged on its side, near a little round window. Sadie's face appeared in the circle of glass, using one finger to point upward. Parker swam to the top of the submarine just in time to see a porthole door swing upward as a bright shaft of light shot out of it, like a lone, stationary searchlight. She swam right up to the submarine hatch and dropped down into the submarine, where the interior was dry as a bone.

She stood up and looked around. The submarine was

filled with crystals and gems—it reminded her of a museum display, just like the ones she wanted to arrange someday. Sadie rushed around the sub, wearing high-heeled shoes and a sundress, her heels clinking and clanging against the metal.

"Emergency! Urgent!" Sadie kept repeating.

"Where's Mom?" Parker asked. "Is she here?"

"It's your fault your mom left!" Sadie said, whipping around to face her.

The submarine began to fill with water, climbing higher and higher. This time, as the water reached her face, Parker found she couldn't breathe it. Arms flailing, she scrambled to the hatch and kept swimming up.

She swam as hard as she could, but she was getting tired and dizzy. She needed to breathe. The closer she got to the surface, the darker things seemed to get.

Suddenly, she reached the surface, breaking through the water into the salty air. She took a deep breath and looked around.

A big white boat appeared in front of her. A giant chile verde–smothered tortilla, spewing scrambled eggs and melted cheese, stood at the helm wearing a little blue captain's hat.

"Aye-aye, Parker. Here's your burrito," said the burrito captain, offering her a little salute. "And I still haven't heard from Sadie."

Parker shot up out of bed and opened her eyes. For a moment, she still saw the ocean surrounding her with its diamond-like blues and rippling waves. But then her eyes cleared and she saw her room at Mountain Harbor, dim and stony and lined with timber. She was as drenched as she'd been in her dream, and as starved for oxygen too. She clutched her chest as she struggled to catch her breath.

"Sorry to wake you," Ellie said. "Weird dream?"

"Talking burrito steering a boat," Parker said. "Pretty normal for me actually."

Ellie chuckled and handed her the plate with the breakfast burrito on it. It looked eerily familiar. Parker felt a little weird eating the burrito that had just talked to her in her dream, but her stomach grumbled loudly and she got over her hesitation quickly.

"Did you say you still haven't heard from Sadie?" Parker asked, though a mouthful of tortilla.

"Ew, don't talk to me when you're chewing," Ellie remarked. "And yes, I said that. Twice. Once before breakfast and just now when I came back in."

Parker swallowed uneasily. "What time is it?" she asked.

"Nine-fifteen," Ellie answered. "Moreau canceled morning session since it was such a late night. We're all supposed to report to her office by ten for task assignments. Also, she says she wants to talk to me and you. In her office. *Again*." Ellie shook her head. "I've never been called to anyone's office in my life before this place," she lamented.

Parker slid out of bed and scurried down the ladder. "Maybe she has news about Sadie!"

"Doubtful. I don't think Sadie wanted Moreau to know she was going anywhere," Ellie said, "so whatever news she might have probably wouldn't be good. Wait—I hope we're not in trouble for not stopping her. But, I mean, she's our aunt. We're just kids. What were we supposed to do?"

"We're not in trouble," Parker insisted, throwing on her uniform in a frenzy of flying fabrics. "Now let's go see what she has to say."

"Aren't you going to eat your burrito?" Ellie asked as Parker grabbed her arm and pulled her out of the room.

"I can't eat that!" Parker said. "It talked to me!"

CHAPTER THIRTEEN

Director Moreau sighed and pinched the bridge of her nose, pushing her glasses up against her thick, dark eyebrows.

"I expected that you two wouldn't be trouble," she said, after seeming to grasp for the right words. "But as you know, I wasn't so sure about your aunt. This is how she was when we were kids here, and this is how she was as an adult Sentry member. And now—" she stopped herself before she could get too carried away. "Never mind. Your aunt's behavior is not your fault, so no need to subject you to my analysis of it. What I do need is for you to tell me where she went."

"We don't actually know," Ellie said.

Ellie caught Parker glancing sideways at her through the corner of her eye.

"But we can assume this has something to do with your mother's disappearance," Moreau said.

"Yes." Ellie nodded.

Parker squirmed in her chair. *She doesn't need to know! We can't trust anyone. Keep it in the family until we hear from Sadie.*

Ellie didn't agree. They needed all the help they could get, and with Sadie gone, Moreau was the sole adult in charge of their well-being. As far as Ellie was concerned, Sadie still hadn't proven herself to be trustworthy, and now she had abandoned them too.

"Wait. Are you saying she was in contact with your mother?" Moreau interrogated.

"Not on a regular basis, as far as I understand," Ellie explained. "But yes. It appears they could text each other in emergencies."

"And your mother"—she made a hand gesture indicating Ellie was welcome to fill in the blank—"texted Sadie? About such an emergency?"

Ellie nodded, prompting Parker to exhale loudly.

"Normally, I wouldn't care what Sadie was up to off-base," Moreau said, leaning forward, her elbows on the desk. "But the fact of the matter is, she stole one of our helicopters. During a time when Mountain Harbor is under the most duress in recent history. The way things are going, we're going to have no choice but to evacuate the premises. And now with only one heli—"

"Wait, what?!" Parker interjected, lunging forward in her chair. "Evacuate? You can't send us away!"

"Parker, I am responsible for the safety of everyone here," Moreau said, calmly, "many of whom—yourselves included—are *children*."

"But we're the reason nobody's gotten hurt yet!" Parker practically shouted, which Ellie had to admit was kind of a good point.

Moreau winced, closing her eyes momentarily as though that might make the whole mess of the last few days disappear. "It will be my call when the time comes. You may be talented, but there are certain risks and responsibilities you are simply not old enough to assume."

Parker huffed and threw her arms across her chest.

"In the meantime, though," Moreau leaned to the side to grab something next to her chair. She held up an elegant backpack, its contents rattling as she placed it on her desk. Ellie recognized it immediately. "I would appreciate you letting me know the moment you hear from Sadie. Though I'm not sure how she plans to contact you, since she left this on the ground near the helipad."

Moreau slid the bag forward toward them. "I thought she might have left some indication of where she was going, but there's nothing I can make sense of. You're welcome to check it out yourself, to see if you can discover anything."

Parker launched out of her chair and snatched up the backpack. She stared at Moreau but didn't say a word.

"And, girls," Moreau said, standing from her chair to tower over both of them in a rather intimidating way, "I want to make myself crystal clear on one last thing: You are under no circumstances to go after your aunt and mother. You will *not* leave this base without my express permission. And if you find out where they are, you will report to me immediately so that *I* may strategize the best way forward. Have I made myself clear?"

"Very," said Parker flatly.

Ellie nodded. "Yes, Director Moreau."

"Thank you," Moreau said, taking her seat again. "Likewise, I shall let you know immediately if I hear anything from your aunt. Which I hope we will, quite soon. We may not always get along, but I care for her, and your mother, deeply."

Ellie swallowed hard. It was heartbreaking enough to think they might not get to rescue their mother. The thought of something happening to Sadie too was just too much.

"You're excused," Moreau said. "Please proceed to the Greenhouse, where I've assigned you to cleanup duty along with my daughters."

Ellie stood and made her way to the door, where Parker's hand was already on the knob.

"Oh. And girls?" Ellie glanced over her shoulder to see Moreau's face overcome with emotion. "Thank you for saving Jules. I will never forget it."

The Greenhouse was a disaster. Plants lay knocked on their sides, pots broken and roots exposed. Leaves and dirt covered every surface while shards of glass were strewn all over the floor. As Ellie surveyed the wreckage, she couldn't believe this was only their third day at Mountain Harbor. It felt like a month's worth of life had happened—and kept on happening.

Jules was already hard at work repotting plants, using her powers to heal their damaged roots, stems, and leaves. Ellie tucked Sadie's backpack on a shelf near the door, for safekeeping, and jumped in to assist. Parker joined Len in sweeping the floors, pushing all the broken glass into one big pile.

Ellie tried to stay focused on her own work but found her thoughts drifting back to Sadie's bag. Had their aunt left it behind on purpose, as a clue? Or was it just an oversight?

She tried to make her distractedness seem like it was coming from somewhere else, which was easy enough in a room full of people with powers. She kept looking up from her lemon trees and aloe plants and berry bushes to watch Len and Parker reconstructing the greenhouse dome. First, they melted the broken shards into molten glass and then—while it floated in midair—shaped it into shiny new windowpanes. They fused each piece together with strips of metal, using alternating blasts of flame and ice.

"All very impressive," Jules muttered to Ellie as she sprinkled some plant food on a potted dwarf banana tree, "but remember who feeds them after all their storms and fireballs." Ellie looked up at Jules, and Jules winked at her through her tortoiseshell cat-eye glasses.

Ellie had to admit, Jules was really starting to grow on her. She had always seemed like someone worth looking up to, but now she seemed like she might also be a potential friend. Together they worked to heal the giant apple tree, lifting it back into its hole and strengthening its roots. Then they focused on the damaged spots, working some plant food and water through its system. *Almost like feeding a baby animal from a bottle*, Ellie thought. After tending to its needs, Jules patted the trunk gently, and Ellie watched as a green light radiated from the bark right where Jules had touched it. She heard rustling in the leaves above and looked up just in time to see a white blossom turn into a shining, pale pink apple. Then, another, right next to it.

Jules giggled. "Aw, thank you, sugar," she purred, patting the tree again, as if it were a cat. She reached up and plucked the two apples from their dainty stems and handed one to Ellie. "She says, 'No, thank *you*.'"

Two ivory blossoms appeared in the exact spots where Jules had accepted the tree's gifts. *No wonder they had so many fruits and vegetables at Mountain Harbor*, Ellie thought, *if Jules can do* this.

By the time lunch rolled around, Ellie wasn't even hungry; Jules had collected enough thank-you gifts from the plants to make an impressive fruit salad and a veggie tray. The two of them had been snacking on apples, berries, bananas, carrots, snap peas, and even peanuts, and when Parker and Len finished soldering the glass wall, they joined Ellie and Jules in snacking.

"Thank you!" Len called, and Ellie knew by her volume and the angle of her chin, tilted up toward the ceiling, that she was thanking the trees and plants, not Jules and Ellie.

"You're welcome, sis," Jules said, a bit coolly.

"Oh, yeah," Len said, through a mouthful of raspberry, "and thanks to you ladies too."

"It was fun!" Parker said, making Ellie reflect on just how different their idea of "fun" had become in recent days.

"Are you guys still going to head over to lunch after this?" Jules asked. "Len and I will walk with you."

Parker shot Ellie a look. *The backpack.*

"Uh, we should probably head back to our room for a bit," Ellie said.

"We're pretty tired," Parker added.

"And we have some things to do. Official, uh, training stuff." Lying was clearly not among Ellie's powers.

Jules cocked her head. "What's going on here?"

Now it was Ellie's turn to shoot Parker a look. Parker didn't answer.

"You may have noticed, but our Aunt Sadie is gone," Ellie

said. Though she wasn't sure if sharing was the right move, it felt really good to get it out in the open. "And not on another one of her whims. I ran into her last night when the alarm was sounding, but she wouldn't tell me where she was headed. All we know is that my mom is in some kind of trouble, and Sadie stole a helicopter to get there."

"Hold on!" Jules shouted, at the exact same moment as Len said, "Wait a second." They glanced at each other, then said in unison, "Your mom is alive?"

"Yeah, as you can imagine, it was a shock to us too," Parker said.

"It's part of the reason we came here," Ellie explained. "To train enough to go rescue our mother. But now apparently Sadie is doing that alone."

"I'm assuming my mom knows about all of this?" Jules asked.

"Ohhh, yes. And she is not amused," Parker said. "We're forbidden from trying to go after them, and the moment we hear from Sadie, we're to report it to her at once." She said the last part while doing her best impression of Director Moreau.

Ellie ran to the shelf to retrieve Sadie's backpack and placed it on the table. "But we don't know how Sadie is supposed to contact us when she left her bag outside in the snow."

Jules twisted her face up into a look of concentration.

"It just seems like something doesn't add up here. How did Sadie manage to take off in the middle of a blizzard? With no one noticing?"

That was an excellent point, Ellie realized. They'd been so focused on the backpack and whether it was a clue she hadn't even stopped to consider how Sadie had pulled that off.

"And now our mom doesn't want to go help them?" Jules shook her head in disbelief. "History aside, Sadie is a legacy member of the Sentry, and Ginny Powers is a legitimate legend. Our duty is to save them. We should all be on our way there right now."

"Unless . . ." Ellie said.

"Unless something is seriously amiss," Len finished.

"So what are you saying?" Ellie's voice sounded as panicky as she felt. "Do you think Sadie is lying to us?"

Jules sighed. "I don't know what's going on, but things have been strange here ever since the three of you showed up. The Danger attacking multiple times—for the first time in decades? It's been like a circus of fear and destruction."

"How do you know it's Sadie's fault?" Parker barked. "Sadie is the *answer*, not the problem. She only wants to help."

"I dunno," Len said, shrugging. "I don't want to start a fight or anything, but something is definitely off about your aunt."

"Blaming and jumping to conclusions won't get us anywhere," Jules cut in. "There is definitely an imbalance at play, but we don't know where it's coming from. What's important is that we get to the bottom of it so we can keep Mountain Harbor, and everyone here, safe. From this moment forward, we need to stick together."

"I agree," Parker said.

"Now, for our next order of business," Jules declared, placing her hands on her hips, "let's see what's in the bag."

CHAPTER FOURTEEN

Parker reached for the zipper on her aunt's backpack, her breath caught in her throat. In all the discussions of the Sentry, the missions, the secret base, Parker had relished the fact that it all seemed quite spy-like. But now that an actual task had fallen in her lap requiring some actual spy-type skills, Parker wondered if she had what it took. Could she piece together this puzzle and plan a stealthy rescue mission? And if she couldn't, what did that mean for her and Ellie? For Sadie and, most of all, Mom?

In one swift movement, she turned the bag upside down, littering the potting table with its contents. A jumble of random objects landed with a series of *thumps* and *clunks*. Sadie's phone made the loudest *thunk* while a flurry of business cards settled over top, like a stream of giant confetti. Jules grabbed one of the cards.

"Sadie Powers, Ecotourism Consultant," she read aloud. "Wow. Cool."

"What's that?" Ellie asked.

"It's like a person who helps plan sustainable travel and tourism practices," Jules explained. "So it won't negatively impact the local nature and native people. And who helps come up with ways to make existing tourism practices more eco-friendly."

Parker remembered Sadie mentioning her work and wished she'd taken the chance to ask Sadie about her career outside the Sentry. She realized that even though she loved to ponder the careers she'd listed in her journal, she didn't really think about adults' jobs unless they were something she already *knew*—like, obviously her teachers were teachers. Obviously their pediatrician, Dr. Shelly, was a doctor. Obviously Glen the mail carrier was a mail carrier.

They began to sift through the pile of typical purse-fillers. Len picked up a tube of magenta lip gloss in one hand and a pair of expensive-looking sunglasses in the other. "It's like she's not even one of us," she remarked.

"It's called fashion, sis," Jules scoffed. "Did you see that pantsuit she wore the first day she was here? With the ruffled blouse?" Len stared blankly as though the words didn't register. "Well, it was gorge. When I'm done with all these missions someday, I plan to wear nothing but designer clothes and glasses too."

"Whatever she was wearing wasn't very practical for hiking up the mountain," Parker remarked. "She even had to stop and change her shoes."

"See?" Len said, gesturing toward Parker. "She gets it."

"Oh my goodness," Ellie said, reaching for something in the pile. It was small and metallic, and Parker gasped as she realized what it was.

"What?" Parker struggled to find her words. "How?"

It was the missing compass.

"I knew it!" Ellie spat, gazing down at the tiny instrument. "I *knew* that Sadie took it. We never should have trusted her."

"Whoa, whoa, whoa—what?" Jules asked.

"Our mom gave us this compass," Ellie explained, "and it went missing from our room. And now here it is, suddenly making an appearance among our aunt's possessions."

"Maybe she did take it," Parker countered, "but we don't know why. Maybe Mom needed it for some reason and asked her to bring it."

"Then why wouldn't she just ask? Why would she steal it?"

Parker had to admit it was suspicious. But something inside her refused to believe that Sadie was in the wrong. "The truth is, we have no way of knowing. But you know who does know? Sadie. And you're in luck! Because if we go find her, you can ask her yourself."

Ellie narrowed her eyes and slid the compass into her pocket.

Desperate to change the topic, Parker reached for the most prominent item on the table—a thick, forest green journal.

Parker flicked it open to a page of geometric sketches. As best as she could tell, the drawings looked like gems, but they were all in some sort of pair, like two shapes stuck together to create one whole.

Parker continued flipping through the journal with her thumb. Some pages were filled to the brim with tidy cursive notes, others with equations, and many others with sketches, like the ones she'd just seen—gemlike shapes that didn't make much sense to her. She turned to the first page and saw a name written in the top right corner in perfect, flowing handwriting. *Barbara Boudin.*

"It's Boudin's journal," Parker said. "And it looks like it has some of her research notes in it."

"Whoa," Ellie remarked, using the same excited tone Parker reserved for things like spy missions. Parker hoped this would help prove that Sadie was on their side, just like Barbara Boudin was.

Parker opened the journal to a page with a gemlike sketch on it and held it up for the rest of them.

"What is that?" Ellie asked, sounding as puzzled as Parker felt.

"It's a chemical compound," Len answered.

"Ah, we haven't taken chemistry yet," Parker said.

"Well, I have, and I still don't know what that is," Len said with a shrug. "It doesn't look familiar and the atoms aren't labeled." Len turned the page and read the wall of notes that followed, muttering under her breath. "Chemical equilibrium . . . carbon sequester—"

"We need Aunt Barb to tell us what all this means," Jules said, shaking her head. "And even if we figure out what all this is, we still might not know what it has to do with where Sadie went."

"Yeah, but we have no idea where Aunt Barb is either," Len groaned.

Jules clicked her tongue. "Aren't you glad to know you're not the only ones with a disappearing aunt?" She laughed wryly, looking first at Ellie, then at Parker.

Len snapped her fingers and her eyes lit up. "We may not have Aunt Barb," she said, "but we *do* have a librarian. Kind of."

"Good thinking!" Jules nodded in agreement. "She's right. We need Gray." She pulled out her phone and tapped the screen until they all heard ringing over the speaker.

"Yes, dear?" Director Moreau's voice emanated through the room.

"Hey, Mom," Jules said sweetly, "we're done in the Greenhouse and we've already eaten lunch. Do you want us to go on patrol now?"

It was quiet for a moment as Moreau considered the question. Finally, she said, "You and Parker didn't get much sleep due to that whole mess last night. Why don't the four of you just take it easy for the next few hours?"

Jules smiled widely at the rest of them. "Sounds good, Mom. So when do you want us to come find you?"

"How about after dinner?" Moreau suggested.

"All right," Jules replied. "We'll come to your office after dinner."

"Thanks, honey," Moreau said. "Love you."

"Love you too!" Jules ended the call. She tapped away with her thumbs, rapid-fire, staring at her screen. "There," she declared. "I just texted Gray to meet us at the library in ten minutes. And not to let my mom see him."

"He won't like that," Len remarked. "You know he doesn't like breaking the rules."

"He's not breaking any rules," Jules said. "He's just doing something that's slightly secret."

"Yeah, well he's not going to like *that* either," Len said with a chuckle.

They made their way to the library, which looked sort of like a cross between a used bookstore and an underground ski lodge. The walls were lined with volumes housed on thick wooden shelves, while a massive chandelier composed of tree branches hung in the center of it all. Jules immediately escorted everyone to the very back of the room, where a velvet sofa sat facing a small TV. "That way, if we get interrupted, we can just say we wanted to go somewhere quiet and watch a movie," she explained.

She clicked on a movie, some sort of nature documentary about the American prairie that Parker guessed was about fifty years old. In a series of grainy images, bison grazed on dry grass while lazy clouds floated overhead. It looked so calm. Parker was surprised to find herself wishing she could travel through the television and into the peaceful scene.

"Perfect," Len joked as she plopped down on the large sofa. "The next time I can't sleep, remind me to come watch this movie. I'm sure it'll do the trick."

"Oh, shush," Jules snapped. "Gray should be here any minute."

As if on cue, Gray popped out from behind the nearest bookshelf. "Oh, I love this one!" he said when his eyes fell on the screen. "I never truly appreciated prairie dog tunnels before I saw it. Did you know their vocabulary is more complex than any other animal language that's been decoded?"

"Really? I didn't know that," Parker said. Now that she thought about it, Gray actually reminded her of a prairie dog. Same sandy colored hair, same energetic disposition, same apparently lengthy vocabulary.

"Well, we're not actually watching this movie, Gray," Jules explained.

"I figured as much," Gray said with a nod. "You wouldn't make me sneak around behind your mom's back to watch a movie. Especially since you know I don't like sneaking around anyone's back, least of all your mother's."

"Yes," Jules said, "I know, and I apologize, but I promise it's worth it."

"I wouldn't have come if I didn't think it was," Gray sighed. "With everything that's gone on the past few days, I figured I needed to come here myself some time and try to make some sense of it. Parker and I even had a hunch we were going to dig into, right, Parker?"

Parker pulled Barb's journal from the knapsack and handed it to him. "Yes, but before we get into that stuff, we need to make sense of *this*."

Gray took the journal from her outstretched hand and opened it to the first page. Suddenly, his whole body language changed. He stood straighter, carefully gripping the book as though he were holding a sacred artifact or a tiny, endangered creature.

"How did you get this?" he asked.

"Aunt Sadie had it in her bag," Parker answered. "She dropped it before she left base, and we're trying to figure out where she went. We thought maybe there were clues in that journal."

Gray began to make his way through the notebook, his eyes

taking a few moments to scan each page. They watched him for a few minutes, the silence punctuated only by the voice of the Western-twanged narrator and the occasional squeaks of prairie dogs from the television in the background. About halfway through the journal, Gray stopped abruptly. "Of *course*!" His eyes went wide. "Of course! It makes perfect sense!"

"What?" Jules demanded. "What makes sense?"

Gray turned the journal to face the group, and Parker immediately recognized the sketches. The pages were packed with drawings of the gemlike shapes, two faceted structures joined into one.

"Twinning," Gray said plainly, a beaming smile consuming the entire lower portion of his face.

"Twinning?" Jules echoed in confusion.

"Something tells me he doesn't mean unintentionally dressing the same as one of your friends," Len said.

"Twinning is a geological term to describe a symmetrical formation composed of two adjacent crystals," Gray explained.

"So they are gems!" Parker uttered.

"Not quite *gems*," Gray said, "but gems *are* crystals. Though not all crystals do this twinning thing. Only some of them."

"Let me guess," Parker said, grabbing her new necklace and holding up the milky pink rock at the end, "is one of them quartz?"

"Bingo," Gray said.

"Wait, isn't that what Finn uses to trap those little Danger things?" Jules asked.

"Yes," Parker and Ellie answered in unison.

Gray handed the journal to Jules, crossed over to the library's desktop computer, and sat down. He quickly typed in a password and made his way to an online database.

"What if it isn't the quartz itself," Gray posited as he pulled up a list of minerals that exhibited twinning, "but the entire concept of *twinning* that weakens the Danger? I mean ... we're all twins, right?"

Everyone exchanged wide-eyed glances but didn't say anything. It made perfect sense. It blew Parker's mind a little bit too.

"Okay," Jules said finally, "but what does that have to do with Ginny and Sadie?"

"Maybe it doesn't," Gray said with a shrug, clicking through links of various minerals.

Something tickled at the back of Parker's brain. What *did* these crystals have to do with Ginny and Sadie?

Jules handed the journal back to Gray. "Well, let's not go down a prairie dog tunnel with this crystal thing. What else is in the journal?"

Gray went back to scanning pages, and Parker studied the computer screen. It was a picture of a gigantic crystal geode, so large that people were standing inside of it. As if someone had forcefully shoved the memory into her skull, the vision of the amethyst room at the museum hit Parker so hard she staggered on her feet.

It was like walking into a giant geode, she remembered her sister saying in their room a few days prior.

A giant geode.

"My mom is in a cave!" Parker blurted out.

Everyone turned to look at her.

"Huh?" Jules asked.

"My mom is in a cave lined with crystals," Parker continued. "With these twinning crystals that weaken the Danger. I'll bet she's been trapped there, sensing it was the only place she was safe."

"If the Danger were after Ginny," Jules questioned, "then would being around a large deposit of these minerals *protect* her?"

"Hypothetically, yes," Gray said with a nod.

"And would a cave have large enough deposits of these minerals?" she asked.

"Absolutely," Gray answered with an emphatic nod. "In fact, many of these minerals are staples of typical karst cave geology."

"You lost me," Len said.

"Okay, let me explain," Gray said, twirling in the computer chair to face them. "Most caves were formed by a gradual erosion of acidic water. That same process actually forms some of these twinning crystals. Calcite, aragonite, gypsum . . ."

"So caves are basically *made* of this stuff?" Len asked.

"I mean, they're mostly limestone," Gray said, "but there are a *lot* of these other minerals present, especially on the surface, since that's where contact with the acidic water would have happened."

"But now for the million-dollar question," Jules said. "Can this information help us find Ginny?"

Gray's triumphant grin faded in an instant.

"What?" Parker asked. "What's wrong?"

"Remember the part where I said *most caves* are formed this way?" Gray questioned.

"Crap," Jules grumbled. "If most caves are like this—"

"We have no way of narrowing it down," Parker finished her thought.

"Except that Sadie told me it would take only a few hours to get to Mom," Ellie stated.

Now they all looked at Ellie, who seemed uneasy that everyone's eyes were on her.

"How far does that narrow it down?" Jules asked, leaning over Gray's shoulder as he swiveled back to face the computer.

"Helicopters travel about a hundred and fifty miles per

hour," he muttered as he typed and clicked. "So, let's say a range of four hundred and fifty miles . . . which would mean about a three-hour flight."

Within a few moments, he had created a map pinpointing all the major caves within four hundred and fifty miles of Granite, Colorado. Parker's stomach dropped when she saw dozens of little orange pins all over the map.

"That's still a lot," Len groaned.

"There has to be something else in this journal," Jules stated, flipping through it with desperation.

"Can't we just track the actual helicopter?" Len grumbled.

"Well, yes and no," Gray answered. "Those helicopters are old enough that they don't have satellites. They do have transponders, so that they can be recognized by radars."

"Great!" Len said, excitedly. "So pull up the radar thing and see where she went!"

"I'm good with computers, but I'm not 'hack the North American Air Traffic Control radar systems' good, Len," Gray stated. "Plus it's probably a federal crime."

"What's a federal crime?"

In unison, they all whipped around to see Finn standing behind them, arms crossed and eyebrows raised. Parker's heart pounded in her ears.

"Uh . . . hacking the Air Traffic Control radar—" Gray started.

"Gray!" Jules said.

"You bunch are trying to find Sadie, aren't you?" Finn asked, crossing to the desk they all huddled around.

"My mom *told* them to," Jules said, pointing at Parker and Ellie.

"Well, if she told Parker and Ellie to look for clues," Finn said gently, "why am I looking at five people and why are they talking about committing federal crimes?"

"Obviously I wasn't going to actually do it," Gray grumbled under his breath. "I don't even know how!"

"We're just helping," Jules replied, placing her hands on her hips and lifting her chin ever so slightly in the air. "Providing reinforcement. Sadie didn't leave much to go on and I thought Parker and Ellie seemed overwhelmed, so I figured we could help them, that's all."

Finn nodded, still looking a bit suspicious. Then their eyes fell on the green journal on the desk in front of Gray.

"What is that?" Finn demanded, pointing at it sharply.

"Aunt Barb's journal," Len answered. "That's all we have to go on."

"*One* of Barb's journals," Finn corrected, moving in closer and snatching it up. "She lent me the rest of them. But this is the first one. This is the *beginning* of her research."

"Well, good, then," Gray said, "maybe you can help us figure out where Sadie and Ginny are."

"Ginny?" Finn echoed in disbelief. "Ginny Powers? Ginny's *alive*?"

Everyone nodded.

"And Sadie is *with* Ginny?" Finn asked.

They all nodded again.

"Well, now I see why you're all so serious about this," Finn said. "All right, tell me what you've got."

"Basically just that Ginny could be in a cave," Jules said. "Because of all the twinning minerals and stuff in the journal and the fact that it weakens the Danger."

"Good, good," Finn remarked, nodding thoughtfully. "Smart thinking. Doesn't narrow it down much."

"We know the cave is only a few hours away," Ellie said, "according to Sadie's estimate of how long it would take her to get there."

"Okay," Finn said. "Better, but still a lot."

"And that's where we're at," Parker concluded.

"I think I can help," Finn said.

"You can?!" they all exclaimed.

Finn nodded. "This entire journal is filled with Barb's initial notes on her theories about what weakens and wards off the Danger. I've spoken to all of you about some of those things in the very recent past. But I'm surprised, Jules, that you don't remember *our* recent conversation about this topic."

Parker watched Jules's eyes go wide with recognition as Finn opened the journal to a sketch of a plant with flower-shaped leaves.

"*Spurge*," Jules gasped.

"Spurge?" Len repeated, pronouncing the word as if it were something gross, which to be fair is exactly how it sounded.

"Leafy spurge, to be exact," Finn said. "Jules and I discussed it just last week when we were collecting noxious weeds for the Botany lesson."

"And the Danger is vulnerable to this spurge?" Ellie asked.

"Yes," Jules said. "It's one of many plants that secrete a milky, toxic fluid to protect itself when injured. Barb believes that this toxin affects the Danger just as negatively as it does the plants' predators."

"So our mom is likely hiding in a cave that's near a bunch of this type of plant?" Parker asked.

"Precisely," Finn answered. They pointed at a section of the map just to the north of Granite. "Leafy spurge has become a predominant noxious weed in the northern United States and into parts of Canada. So we're looking at North Dakota, South Dakota, Montana, Wyoming . . ."

Gray zoomed in on the area Finn had pointed out. There were still quite a few caves to choose from.

"That's what, seven caves?" Parker stared at the screen, feeling slightly defeated.

"Can we divide and conquer?" Jules asked. "Split up into pairs and search a few of them?"

"I suppose we could," Finn answered. "But we probably don't need to. Because I know exactly which one Sadie went to."

"*What*?" Len asked.

"How?" Jules and Gray demanded.

"Because the helicopters may be too old to have satellites, but they each have a satellite phone on board," Finn stated. "I bought them a few months ago. Satellite phones can be tracked by their GPS units, and I have all of that information right *here*." They pulled their phone out of their back pocket and waved it around with glee.

"So you've known where Sadie was this whole time?" Jules asked, sounding more than a little annoyed.

Finn nodded. "Yep."

"You know," Gray sighed, "you could have just said that."

"I could have," Finn replied, "but this was *way* more fun."

CHAPTER FIFTEEN

For the rest of the afternoon, they all did their bests to play it cool—something Ellie was admittedly not very good at. The plan was to go after Ginny and Sadie that night, without alerting the director. Finn very reluctantly agreed to help with transportation and even more reluctantly swore that they wouldn't tell Moreau. The girls would take off after dinner, and Jules, Len, and Gray would stay on base and cover for them.

"Just act like everything's normal," Jules instructed.

But everything *wasn't* normal, Ellie thought as she picked at her veggie burger. This was her last meal before she attempted to rescue her mother. There was nothing remotely normal about that.

Even though the mission was obviously worth it, and though she knew that time was of the essence, Ellie felt unsettled that their plan would happen in secret. She wished they had the full support of the Sentry behind them, along with the backup and intelligence that would bring. As far as rescue missions went, she felt unprepared. They had barely started their training, never mind completed it. They had no idea what was waiting for them there. Despite what Parker said, they weren't even sure if they could trust Sadie! And then there was the issue of the Danger, which always left them scrambling.

Over the last six years, there had been a lot of moments when Ellie had wished she could talk to her mother. She wanted her mom's advice on everything from navigating middle school to making friends to managing her dad and Parker. Since discovering her powers, that feeling had only intensified.

Until now, Ellie's only choice was to accept the fact that her mom's advice was not available. So for as long as she could remember, she'd tried her best to imagine it. With every choice she made, every action she took, she tried to do whatever she thought would make her mom proud. Right now, she didn't know if her mom would condone sneaking around and breaking the rules, but she hoped she would be proud of their bravery.

"C'mon, Ellie," Parker said, interrupting her thoughts. "You ready?"

Ellie didn't know how to answer that. Could she ever be ready?

"I get it," Parker said, nodding. Then she pressed a little package into Ellie's hand. It was a packet of trail mix, from the pantry. "I figured you'd be too nervous to eat, so take that in case you get hungry later."

"Thanks," Ellie said, feeling slightly comforted for the first time that day.

"Everything is going to be fine," Parker said, placing a reassuring hand on her shoulder. "Like, more than fine. Imagine how good we'll feel this time tomorrow when all of this is behind us."

"We don't know that." Ellie sighed.

Parker opened her mouth to respond, but Jules sidled up to her and beat her to it.

"It's time," Jules said. "Finn told my mom they're leaving for a Fountainhead run nearby, so the sooner, the better."

Parker nodded as Jules led them out of the mess hall, down the hall, toward her mother's office. Ellie trudged after them, feeling disconnected from what was happening, almost like she was watching a movie about her own life.

A couple times when she was younger, Ellie's dad had made some remark about not remembering how he drove from one point to another. He'd pick them up from school and when they pulled into the driveway, he'd say, "Whoa! That's a little scary. Don't even remember driving here!" Ellie never had any idea what he was talking about. But when she reached Moreau's office a few minutes later, she realized this was *exactly* what he had meant. Somehow, Ellie's feet had just trekked through the winding corridors of the base without her brain registering a single second of it.

Jules ushered them farther through the tunnels until they were safely out of earshot. "Can you two get to the helipad from here?" she whispered.

"Yes," Parker murmured.

"Then good luck," Jules said, squeezing their shoulders. "The whole base is counting on you. And we've all got your back." She nodded abruptly, then turned and walked away.

Parker took a deep breath and grabbed Ellie's hand. "Ready?"

Ellie wanted to shake her head from side to side. But that wasn't an acceptable answer. She supposed there were some things she'd never feel ready for, but that wasn't a reason not to try. Ellie swallowed hard and squeezed her sister's hand as an image of her mother's face floated into her mind.

She nodded. "As ready as I'll ever be."

When they reached the helicopter, Finn was waiting with packs for each of them. "Okay. We've got snacks, canteens, head lamps, night vision goggles—"

"Whoa!" Parker said.

"I know, right?" Finn chuckled. "Feels like a spy movie, huh?"

"Exactly!" Parker exclaimed.

The girls took their seats as Finn readied the helicopter for takeoff.

"We're headed to a cave not too far from here, relatively speaking, on the south end of South Dakota. Get comfy. It'll be about an hour."

In practice, that hour went by faster than the walk from the mess hall to the helipad. Ellie barely realized they were en route when Finn announced they were preparing to land.

The helicopter hovered, then settled to the ground with a gentle thud. The blades slowed, their constant whirl giving way to a steady *chop-chop-chop*, until they finally stopped altogether.

Finn gave the all-clear signal, and Ellie hopped out and slung her pack over her shoulders. There was still plenty of light in the sky, though she could see the haziness of dusk tinting the clouds above them. Then she realized that they weren't clouds, at all. It was the Danger, hovering above the park, swirling in a pattern that looked to Ellie like a figure eight.

"I did some research on this place in between the library and dinner," Finn said as the three of them approached what looked like a rocky hill. "There's an entrance just ahead, but it doesn't get used for public tours because it's narrow and hard to navigate. Apparently, it's also home to a large population of bats that the park tries not to disturb for conservation reasons. But Sadie landed pretty close to here, so I'm thinking that's the route we should take."

Public tours, Ellie thought to herself, her eyes shifting back to the Danger hovering above. "Can't they see it?" she asked, pointing upward. "Don't all the people who come to the cave wonder what the heck is going on?"

"The Danger?" Finn clarified. "No. The average person can't see it—well, not how *we* see it, anyway. They can see what it causes—weather, fire, destruction. They would have seen the blizzard on the mountaintop. They see the storms and the chaos it leaves in its wake. But only those of us with powers have the awareness to see it in this form."

Ellie wondered how many terrible things she had seen on the news in recent years—the hurricanes and tornadoes and earthquakes and mudslides—that could have been caused by the Danger. She shuddered.

As they neared the hilly formation, Ellie could make out a jagged opening in one of the rocks. Her eyes kept flicking upward to check on the Danger, and she could see that Parker and Finn were doing the same thing. But the Danger didn't seem to notice them at all, even when they were standing directly beneath it at the cave entrance.

"I'll stay near the entrance and keep an eye on this thing," Finn said, pointing toward the smoky cloud. "The cave isn't all that big—its overall footprint is smaller than the tunnels at Mountain Harbor—so I'm confident you can manage. As soon as I see you at the entrance, I'll run ahead and get the chopper going."

The twins grasped hands. Parker nodded and Ellie took a deep breath.

"Thank you, Finn," Parker said.

"I know you two can do it," Finn said. "I've seen you in action and I have no doubts. If I had, I would have tattled on you to Moreau and let her deal with this." They cracked a smile. "Now, go get your mom."

Parker headed into the opening, and Ellie followed close behind. For a minute, they traversed the narrow, rocky passage in silence. Ellie was surprised at how quickly the shred of light from outside disappeared and they were plunged into total darkness. They turned on their headlamps, which made Ellie feel less like a spy and more like a cartoon mole, who were seemingly always drawn wearing lamps just like these.

The walls around them shimmered with a milky, moonlike sheen that served only to amplify the brightness. Ellie's body was suddenly flooded with a feeling of annoyance.

What this! Her head filled with a teeny, raspy squeak. It was immediately joined by another, then another, forming a chorus of little angry voices.

I was a-sleeping. But now I is awake.

Verrrry awake.

BRIGHT!

Bad bad bad bad bad bad bad.

Make stop the light! I do not like.

"Parker!" Ellie whispered. Parker whipped around to face her. Now Parker's light was in *her* eyes. The voices were right; it was annoying. She held up a hand to block the beam. "Don't look up with your head lamp on."

"Why?" Parker asked.

"The bats are trying to sleep," Ellie explained. "They don't like it."

"Oh," Parker said apologetically. "That makes sense. Sorry, bats!"

They started to walk again. Parker ran her hand along the smooth wall.

"Do you hear anything? From the rocks?"

Parker shook her head. "No. Hey, maybe you could ask the bats for some intel! Like in *Anastasia*."

"They're trying to sleep," Ellie rebutted.

"Okay, but if Mom is in here, I'm sure they know her," Parker said. "And if they know her, I'm guessing they wouldn't mind helping."

Ellie sighed. "Okay, here goes." She cleared her throat, but when she opened her mouth, she couldn't bring herself to raise her voice above a soft murmur. "Hi! Um, bats? I'm sorry to disturb you, but we're searching for our mother and we're wondering if you can help." She poured all her concentration into sending the bats her message, communicating through her energy how grateful she would be.

A shudder swept across the top of the cave passage. It sounded like a gust of wind rustling through hundreds of dry, autumn leaves. Ellie desperately wanted to see them but kept her head down so as not to shine her light in their eyes.

Suddenly, she felt a rush of air by her right ear.

Arm please! Came a squeaky little voice. It was easily the most adorable thing Ellie had ever heard. *Hold out arm, okay?*

She did as she was told and felt two little sets of claws clutch her hoodie sleeve. Instinctively, she pushed the button to extinguish her light, but it didn't shut off. Instead, the color flipped to red.

Ah! Is better.

In the soft, scarlet glow, Ellie studied the bat hanging from her arm. It looked nothing like the monstrous creatures she'd seen in movies or on Halloween decor. For one thing, it was tiny, maybe three inches long including its humongous, pointy ears. Its black wings were so thin they looked almost like stockings, and its face was covered in a light brown fuzz.

You here to look for lady? the bat asked.

It reminded Ellie a bit of a toddler, high-pitched and with a loose grasp of pronouns. But for a cave-dwelling creature who must not encounter many humans, its communication skills were quite impressive.

"Yes, we are," Ellie said. "Two ladies, actually. One is my mother, who may have been here for a while. The other is my aunt, who would've joined last night. Have you seen them?"

Yes, yes! I seen. Original lady here verrrrrrrry long time. I help lady. She help me. Lots of helping. Is good at understanding bats, the lady is.

Sounded like Ginny Powers.

"How do you help her?" Ellie asked.

I brings her little plants. I eat the beetles so they no eat the plants. That way plants can grow more. The lady likes the plants, even though plants is gross—blech! The bat made a series of dramatic gagging sounds to demonstrate its point. *Beetles is tasty. But this way everybody wins. Well, everybody but beetles, I guess.*

"I think the bats help Mom grow leafy spurge," Ellie muttered.

"*Spurge.* What is with that plant's name?" Parker groaned.

"And how does the lady help you?" Ellie asked, ignoring her sister.

The lady she heals us. Many bats is sick during big sleep. Too much happens is bad for bats so no sleeping! The noses get white. When happens we can't breathe. But the lady clean our noses so we no die.

"That sounds like her," Ellie said, nodding.

The lady help our babies grow big. She tells me someday her babies come save her like she saves us. You Lady's babies? Is big for babies.

"Yes," Ellie said, giggling. Parker looked at her as though Ellie had completely lost her mind. "We're her babies, but we're older now. And we're here to help her, like she said."

We love Lady, the bat squeaked. *I be sad if the lady is leaving, but happy if she gets to see babies and leave black cloud that make her sick. Cloud always here. Cloud always waiting. Cloud never go.*

The Danger was hovering there for *Ginny*, Ellie realized. It didn't care about them because it only wanted her.

"The Danger is just here for her," Ellie told Parker, "The bat says it never leaves. And it sounds like it's draining her."

"I thought it was weird that it didn't seem to care about us," Parker commented. "Although I thought it was supposed to be random and unpredictable. Since when does it care about anything?"

"Yeah, it is weird," Ellie muttered.

There was something about all this that didn't add up. The Danger was supposed to be chaotic and mindless, according to Moreau. But it seemed that this had a mind of its own, an actual goal, an actual plan.

"Where is the lady now?" Ellie asked, pushing the Danger out of her thoughts.

Deeeeeeeeeep in cave. Deeper than bats go for sleep. She come up here to get the plants then goes back to shiny room. That is where she sleep.

"Shiny room," Ellie repeated. "It sounds like she must stay in a room with the crystals she needs for protection."

You go find the lady and I need to go food soon anyway. You keep going and you gets to shiny room. Okay?

"Okay. Thank you for your help," Ellie said.

Oh yes nice person I thank you too. Lady named me Samira, you can call me Samira.

"Thank you, Samira," Ellie said, prompting Parker to give her another skeptical look.

Bye-bye Lady's babies!

Ellie felt the little claws release their grasp on her hoodie, then heard the faintest of flutters as the bat flitted away. Ellie made a silent resolution to come back and check on Samira as often as possible whenever this mess was finished. She barely had time to finish her thought before she heard the rustling of *many* bats overhead.

"Where are they going?" Parker asked as the force of their little wings together created a soft breeze.

"It must be twilight," Ellie said. "Samira said—" before she could get the rest of the words out, the sound of tumbling rocks echoed through the narrow passageway before them. She and Parker flipped their headlamps back to the brightest setting and slowly continued in the direction of the sound.

"Um, Ellie?" Parker sounded more concerned than Ellie had ever heard her. "These aren't the kind of caves with bears in them, right? I mean, wouldn't Finn have said so?"

"I dunno. But they probably wouldn't give tours here if it was full of angry bears." Ellie stumbled over some uneven rocks, grasping at the tunnel wall to steady herself.

"Can you talk to bears?" Parker prattled on. "Like if one was going to attack us, you could tell it that we want to be friends?"

"Parker."

"Yes?"

"Look."

Both girls stared straight ahead, hardly believing what they saw.

CHAPTER SIXTEEN

The form was headed directly at them. For a few long moments, the twins stood frozen, listening to the crunch of gravel grow louder with every advancing step.

"Hello?"

Parker stopped cold. She would know that voice anywhere.

"Mom?" she said, in a tiny voice.

"Girls?"

Parker stood, frozen, unsure of what to do or say. It felt like her birthday and the first day of school and her first-ever school dance and the Ultimate Frisbee Championships, all rolled into one. It was everything she'd ever wanted, the moment she'd imagined and anticipated for as long as she could remember. But now that it was happening, it almost didn't feel real.

"Mom!" Ellie cried, as Ginny's face appeared in the lamplight. Improbably, she looked exactly the same. A little more tired, perhaps, and covered in a lot more dirt than the last time they'd seen her. But she was unmistakably their mother, with the same wise, caring eyes, the same long black hair, the same smile that lit up whenever she saw them.

"My babies!" their mother cried, running forward to engulf them both in her arms. "You don't know how much I've missed you," she said, burying her face in her daughters' hair. "There were so many times when I worried this day would never come."

"I knew it would," Parker said, her face pressed against her mom's jacket. "I always said we would find you one day." The fabric smelled like plants and dirt and musty earth, but more than that, it smelled like *her*, that familiar smell she had missed so much. When Ginny first disappeared, Parker would sometimes slip into her mom's closet and close the door, hiding among her things. It was the easiest way she'd found to feel close to her mother, enveloped by her. But nothing could come close to the real thing. She felt something roll down her cheek and realized she was crying.

"Let me get a look at you," Ginny said, stepping back to hold them at arm's length. She was beaming and crying. "I have so much to ask you! I have so much to say. But first, I take it we should probably get out of here." She snapped back into mom mode. "How did you get here? Are you here with the director? You didn't travel alone, did you?"

Another set of footsteps crunched into the narrow chamber. Parker looked beyond her mom to see Sadie coming into the lamplight. Their normally glamorous aunt looked even more identical to their mother, with dirt streaked on her clothing, her black hair askew. Her normally made-up face glistened with sweat. Before Ellie could possibly say anything, Parker rushed over and tackled her aunt in a hug. Sadie grunted at the impact and then laughed.

"I'm glad you're okay, Aunt Sadie," Parker said as they separated.

"So am I," Sadie replied, drawing Parker close. "I was hoping you'd find us."

"Did you drop your bag on purpose?" Parker asked, hearing how utterly ridiculous it sounded, even as she said it. "So that we'd follow the clues?"

"No," Sadie admitted. "It was never my plan to lure you here. But then the bag blew out of the helicopter and I couldn't circle back to get it without being seen."

"I told you," Ellie remarked to Parker.

"Well," Parker sighed, "you were right."

"So I took my chances, because I was confident you'd do the right thing. Which you did, by asking for help. Knowing when to get help is an underutilized power, if you ask me—I'm glad you girls were wise enough to try it."

"I have one more question," Ellie said. "Why did you take the compass?"

"What compass?" Sadie said.

Ellie produced the compass from her own pocket and held it in her palm. It spun around a full turn before stopping and pointing directly at Ginny.

"The compass I left for you!" their mother said, instantly recognizing it.

"Someone stole it from our bunk," Ellie said, accusingly. "And then we found it in Sadie's backpack."

"Then someone must have put it there," Sadie said. "Because I've never seen it before."

Parker fully believed her, and she hoped Ellie did too. Although she supposed that at this moment, she didn't really have a choice.

"Look, I'm sure we can get to the bottom of it once we're back at base," Sadie said. "But we have more pressing matters ahead of us. Unfortunately, we're not out of the woods yet." She drew back and straightened her shoulders, her mouth drawing into a resolute line.

"So, what's the plan?" Parker asked. "Finn is waiting near the entrance with the other helicopter at the ready. Do we make our getaway?"

"So grown up," their mother murmured, shaking her head in disbelief.

Sadie pointed to Ginny's pack. "Your mom and I are each carrying a water bladder full of a toxin that will weaken the Danger."

"The leafy spurge milk?" Ellie said.

"How did you know that?" Ginny asked, astonished.

"Barb's journal," Ellie replied. "And also, Samira told me."

"Ah," Ginny said with a chuckle, "you met Samira. I thought you might. She *loves* to talk."

"As soon as we emerge, we douse the Danger with as much of the milk as we can. The Danger hates the toxin, but it won't overpower it entirely. It will only *weaken* it," Sadie continued. "So we can't rely on that alone."

"So, you're saying we'll have to use our powers to defeat it?" Ellie asked.

"I'm saying we'll have to move quickly and stay alert. And yes, do whatever we need to in order to get away safely." Sadie paused. "But with both of you here, our chances of overpowering it are much greater."

They steadily made their way toward the cave's entrance, Parker's heart beating louder with every step.

"Now remember, we don't want to disturb the ecosystem too much," Ginny said, sounding exactly the way Parker had always remembered—calm, collected, and above all, conscientious. Especially when it came to the environment. "That means no granite bombs, Parker. Nothing that could harm any of the nearby wildlife."

"You told her about that?" Parker looked at her aunt.

"Of course I did! How could I not?"

The entrance was visible up ahead, the last slivers of twilight slanting through the narrow opening. What else was waiting for them out there?

"So, I'm guessing fire is out of the question?" Parker asked.

"Yes, fire is probably best avoided," their mom confirmed.

"How about lightning?"

Ginny thought for a moment. "Lightning is okay, as long as it's confined to the sky. No ground strikes. And absolutely no hitting trees."

"Got it," Parker said.

They stopped just inside the opening, taking a moment to ready themselves for whatever waited outside.

"Girls, you and I will step out first and get into position," Sadie said. "As soon as your mom appears, the Danger will respond, so we have to be ready."

They nodded. A flicker of worry played across Ellie's face, but it passed just as quickly as it appeared.

"It's going to be all right," their mother said, looking them both in the eye. "But before we go out there, I want you to know that I love you. And I'm proud of you. No matter what happens, nothing could possibly make me any prouder, or more grateful, than I am right now." She paused, taking a moment to drink them both in, before asking, "Are you ready?"

"Yes," the twins answered in unison. Even without the gift of telepathy, Parker could tell they both meant it.

Outside the cave, the evening seemed suspiciously calm. The amber glow of twilight had all but vanished, replaced with the amethyst sky of early night. In the dim light, Parker saw some of the tiny cave bats dart out of the rocks and flit over toward the tree line where they'd landed. Speaking of landings, Parker thought as she scanned the grounds, Finn was nowhere to be seen. She hoped they were okay. Was it possible they'd already seen the group coming and run ahead to the chopper? Either way, she couldn't dwell on it. They had to keep moving.

Ellie and Parker got into position on either side of the cave's entrance. Sadie emerged behind them, placing her pack full of toxin on the ground.

The Danger loomed in the sky above them like a swarm of angry bees. When they'd arrived, it had been moving in a figure eight pattern, but now it darted haphazardly in all directions. It reminded Parker of when their neighbor had gotten a drone for Christmas last year, but piloting it proved to be too much for his kindergarten fingers. It had looped and shaken and swerved all over the air between their houses until eventually it met its demise in a nearby shrub.

"Ready!" Sadie called, and Ginny emerged from the cave. As soon as she was out in the open, the Danger let out an ear-splitting roar.

"Now!' Ginny shouted, as the cloudy monstrosity dove from the sky, headed straight for her. She grabbed the small hose attached to her pack and began to spray the cloud with the toxin. Sadie picked up her bag full of liquid and lobbed it into the cloud, like a giant, poisonous water balloon.

Parker marveled at how the creature shrieked and wailed and writhed, ultimately shrinking to half of its size. But still, it continued to rage.

"Now, Parker!" Sadie called, as Ginny took off running in the direction of the helicopter.

The Danger roared as it tried to regain its size. Parker jutted her hands out in front of her, palms facing the creature. Her bracelet grew hot against her wrist. Electricity crackled in her fingertips, then spread to her whole palms. White heat shot out in a giant trident, striking the Danger in its quivering core. With a mournful howl, the black smoke dissipated for a moment. Its tentacles grasped feebly at the air, as though it was trying to catch its breath.

"Ellie!" Ginny called, raising her voice above the howl. "Just inside the tree line over to our right, there's a giant patch of spurge. Grab as much as you can, pull the tops off all of it, then send it over to Parker."

Parker looked at her sister from the corner of her eye, keeping her focus on the Danger in front of her.

"You said not to disturb the nature—" Ellie started.

"The spurge is already disturbing the nature, remember?" Ginny said. "We're lucky the spurge is here, but it's not *supposed* to be here. The rangers have spent decades trying to get rid of it. You'd be doing them a big favor."

Ellie needed no further encouragement. She took off into the trees, moving faster than Parker had ever seen her run. Parker placed all her focus on holding the Danger at bay, keeping the wind swirling in a steady cyclone around it.

Then, she heard what sounded like a thousand tiny branches snapping all at once. Within a matter of seconds, a ribbon of plant toxin snaked through the night sky, headed toward her outstretched hands. But before it could get there, it was swept up by the wind. The toxin swirled around the vortex, closer and closer to the center, until it reached the Danger's smoggy body.

Parker had never heard a sound quite like the Danger when the second round of toxin hit it, but she knew it was the last sound this particular creature would ever make. With one final shudder, its darkness dissolved, its core cracked, its tentacles shuddered and snapped back into the shrinking cloud.

As the ribbon of toxin finished its swirling dance, Parker knew this was her shot. She let the air grow calm. Then she waited.

The Danger groaned and stretched one last thrashing black tentacle toward Ginny. But Parker was ready. She unleashed the current that had been forming between her hands, watching as it leapt straight to the Danger's weakened core. It broke apart, silently sputtering into a pile of ash.

"YES!" Ginny hollered into the night. "We did it!"

Sadie whooped and clapped her hands. Ellie ran back into the clearing, smiling widely and laughing. Parker just grinned. She was too out of breath to cheer, and her hands were too exhausted from conjuring lightning and wind to clap along with the others. But she could join as the four of them danced in celebration—of Ginny's freedom, of their togetherness, of their freedom from the Danger at long last.

CHAPTER SEVENTEEN

Two arms grabbed her from behind, causing Ellie to jump. "That was amazing!"

"Finn!" she yelled, turning to face them. Relief flooded her body. They were safe!

"Where were you?" asked Parker. "We were worried!"

"Oh, you know, just hiding out near the helicopter," Finn said. "I got some strange interference on the satellite phone that I wanted to investigate. Not to mention a pretty irate call from base."

Uh-oh. They'd been so ecstatic about defeating the Danger, Ellie had almost forgotten about the other, slightly less menacing presence waiting for them when they returned.

"I'm sure she was thrilled," said Sadie, her voice dripping with sarcasm.

"Eh, but who doesn't love a reunion?" said Ginny. "It'll all be water under the bridge the moment we get back there. So, how's it looking? Are we clear for takeoff?"

"Yes, but there's been a slight change of plans." Finn smiled sheepishly.

"What?" Parker uttered.

"We're not going back to base."

"Like, ever?" Ellie was aghast. She figured Moreau would be peeved, but she never expected they'd get kicked out of the Sentry.

Finn laughed. "No, we're going back all right. We're just making another stop along the way."

"Oh, phew." Ellie let out a sigh of relief, though it appeared she'd been the only one who was worried.

"There is a big storm not too far from here," Finn said. "On the plains. Flash flooding, funnel clouds—thousands of animals will die if we don't do something. Since we have both the helicopters, and since I wasn't really in a position to refuse a request from Moreau . . ."

"We're the lucky bunch who gets to go," Sadie finished.

"Ding-ding-ding!" Finn exclaimed, pointing a finger at Sadie. "You win a prize!"

"All right," Sadie said, sighing. "Shoot me the coordinates. I'll take the other chopper and meet you there." And with that, she slung her pack over her shoulder and strode toward her helicopter.

"What a day," Parker groaned. "You get reunited with

your long-lost mom and you still have to go on an extra mission!"

"Remember when you couldn't wait to go out on missions?" Finn joked.

"Yeah, a lot can change in a couple days," Ellie said.

"I'll say," Ginny agreed. "I guess we have a lot to catch up on, huh?"

For years, Ellie had kept a running mental list with question after question she wanted to ask her mother. She wanted to know about her mom's work, the precise moment she fell in love with their dad, about their extended family. More recently, she wanted to ask her about Haven, about the Sentry, about her own experience as a twin. She had so many questions that she could probably easily keep her mom talking for a whole week straight. But now that her mother was right there, in front of her, she couldn't think of a single one.

Luckily, Ginny could think of a few.

"How is Dad doing?"

"Um, you know, he's pretty much a normal adult," Parker said.

That prompted a laugh from their mother. "A normal adult? Like one without powers?"

"Yeah, and one who eats boring foods, forgets where he puts all of the stuff he needs every day—phone, wallet, keys—and gets stressed out and starts mumbling and then when you ask what's wrong, says 'Oh, nothing for you to worry about. Adult stuff.'"

"Ah, I see," Ginny nodded. "Normal adult."

"He worries a lot," Ellie added.

"Well," Ginny replied, smiling, "that just makes him a normal *parent*. Sadie told me he's on assignment in Amsterdam this summer?"

"Yeah, he almost didn't take it, but then when he heard we'd be away, he figured he might as well go," Ellie explained, then added, "He misses you a lot."

"I miss him too," their mom said, getting a little choked up. "I can't wait to see him."

"Mom?" Parker ventured. "So, uh, what happened? Why were you gone for so long? And why couldn't you be in touch? Was it the Danger, or . . ." she trailed off.

Ginny sighed. "How did much did Sadie tell you?"

"Not much," Ellie said, looking to Parker for support.

"Basically nothing," Parker confirmed. "Just that both of you were attacked long ago and that she got away and didn't think you survived. And that you've been trapped ever since."

"That's the gist of it," Ginny said. She paused before continuing, and Ellie got the feeling that whatever had happened was difficult for her mother to talk about. She wondered if it might be equally difficult to hear.

"It was six years ago. I got a call about a big storm at Haven. It was worse than anything they'd seen before, and they needed everyone to pitch in and help. I'd left you at home with Dad because as much as I hated being separated, that seemed like the safest option. The day we arrived, Sadie and I were right outside of Haven, just beyond the fence on the road in, when the Danger descended out of nowhere."

The girls sat, rapt. Ellie couldn't help but think how wild it was to be with their mom—their mom—*and* to be discussing something like the Danger.

Ginny took a deep breath, remembering. "Sadie managed to knock it back with a chain of lightning, but the Danger was so strong, it took all her power just to keep it at bay. We tried to run while it was weakened, and Sadie made it to the other side of the wall, but I was a few paces behind where she was and I slipped in the mud. It was the difference of a few seconds, but that was all the Danger needed to pick me up and drag me away."

"It picked you up?" Parker gasped. "Like with its tentacles?"

"First it carried me in a gust of wind and then everything went black. I thought for sure that was it." Ginny shook her head. "Everything I'd learned led me to believe there was no surviving it if it grabbed you."

"And then what happened?" Ellie could barely breathe.

"I woke up in the woods. But it wasn't the woods near Haven."

"Where was it?" Ellie asked.

"I had no idea, but I eventually figured out it was the Yukon," Ginny answered gravely.

"Whoa," Parker breathed. "How did you survive?"

"I was lucky it was summer, otherwise I might've frozen to death. But I knew how to live off the land. Fresh water was easy to come by because of all the glacier runoff, and I could forage for berries and sometimes catch the occasional fish. I tried to find caves to sleep in, even it meant I had to sweet talk some black bears into sharing." She chuckled softly. "And finally, I came across a town—more of an outpost, really—where I stayed for a month trying to get back on my feet. I was so out of it following the attack that I couldn't access my memory. I wasn't able to tell anyone who I was, where I came from, or who they should call."

"The Danger can take people's memories?" It was bad enough that the Danger could cause physical harm, but the thought that it could climb inside someone's mind scared Ellie more than anything.

"It was more like it sapped me of my energy. Like I became

so drained that I couldn't access myself," Ginny explained. "Eventually, my memories did come back. And as I started to piece together where I came from, I tried to make my way back to you. But the Danger wouldn't have it."

"What do you mean?" Parker said.

"The closer I got to you—even if I tried to reach out to you—*things* would start happening. Storms. Electric shocks. One time, an earthquake. I still don't understand it. None of it follows anything I'd been taught about the Danger being random and chaotic. But it's like the Danger—*my* Danger—had a mind of its own."

A shiver ran up Ellie's arms, covering her skin in goose bumps. It was like everything they had said about the Danger's recent attacks at base. It seemed like it was after them. Like it had a mind and a goal and a plan.

"One day, I finally managed to make it to Harborville without mayhem erupting. It was a Saturday morning, and I knew you girls would be at soccer, so I planned to surprise you afterward. But as I got closer to the fields, the winds kicked up around me."

"I remember that!" Parker exclaimed. Ellie did too. She was overcome with sadness thinking that her mom had been so close, but they'd never even known.

"It nearly turned into a hurricane," Ginny said. "Until I started to move away, and then finally, it relented." Her face fell. "I was horrified that so many people could've been hurt just from my attempting to be near you. Eventually, I figured it was safest for everyone if I gave up trying."

Everyone fell silent.

Ellie finally understood all the *whys* behind their mom's absence, something she'd spent years thinking she would never know. What she hadn't expected was that learning the truth would also come with its own form of sadness. Not only for her, but for their mother, who had tried to be there but was forced to stay away, all alone.

There had been so many moments when Ellie had wished her mom could have been there. To see them off on the first day of school, to help with her project for the science fair, to watch Parker catch the winning pass. Ellie had felt like *they* were the ones who missed out. But now she saw it went both ways. Through no fault of her own, her mom had missed out on those moments too.

"Oh, girls," Ginny said, her voice strained, "I am so, so sorry. For everything."

"Mom," Parker murmured, "it wasn't your fault!"

"Now that I see how much you've grown . . . how much I've missed," she said honestly, "I wish I had never gone up to Haven that day. I wish I had split from the Sentry when you were still little. I knew there were some risks involved, but I never thought it would lead to something like this."

"You made a choice to keep us safe," Ellie said. "At every

step of the way, you did what you thought was best. And that's really all any of us can do, right?"

Ginny began to laugh and cry at the same time, tears running down her cheeks as a smile spread across her face. "Oh my goodness," she remarked. "Has your father done an incredible job with you two, or what?"

"He's pretty all right," Parker joked. "Oh! Speaking of Dad, we were supposed to let him know when we found you!"

"Let's call him when we get back to base," Ginny said. "I imagine he's going to have some questions."

Ellie climbed out of the helicopter and stepped into what felt like a world of water. Her feet were fully submerged, and though her boots were waterproof, the waterline went up to her shins, soaking her pants. Each step felt like a cross between climbing and swimming, unsure of what her foot might land on under the water's surface. The ground beneath her shifted, a quagmire of unpredictable mud and sediment. The rain beat down on her as the wind whipped around her face. Thunder rumbled in the distance.

"If lightning hits this floodplain," Sadie said, sloshing through the field, "we're all in big trouble!" Though she was only a couple feet away, she kept her volume at a near-yell to be heard over the wind.

"So are all those cows!" Ellie shouted, pointing to the far end of the pasture where a large herd of cattle stood huddled under a grove of tall trees.

"And all the other wildlife, for that matter," Ginny added. "We need to move the animals to higher ground!"

Sadie pointed to a barn perched on a rocky hill. Ellie thought it looked sturdy enough, holding its own against the ferocious winds. "Up there should hopefully be high enough!"

"What do we do about the flooding?" Ellie asked, having to shout over the thunderous weather. "If it keeps going like this, it's going to spread to all the surrounding pastures. We'll never be able to move all the animals in time!"

"We'll have to move the water!" Ginny declared. "Parker, can you do that?"

"I think so!" Parker answered. "But where do I move it *to*?"

"There's a water tower at the far north end of this field," Finn said. "I saw it when we were coming in." They gestured to their left, where a white dome peeked out above the tops of tall cottonwoods.

"Let's get moving!" Ginny said. "Sadie and I will work on moving the animals. You girls get the water to the tower!"

Parker nodded and took off in a dash, water splashing all around her. Ellie ran after her, her legs burning after only a few bounds. With the water adding so much resistance and the earth shifting with her every step, it felt like she was running through quicksand.

The water tower grew taller the closer they got to it, until eventually it seemed to touch the sky.

Parker reached the base before she did and immediately jumped onto the little metal ladder that led to the top.

"Are you sure we want to be climbing that thing?" Ellie called. What was the use of having powers, she reasoned, if you still had to act like a person? With so much running and climbing, who would have the energy to move the water and the earth?

"Yes!" Parker called back, already a few rungs high. "It'll be more effective if we can look inside. I want to know what we're dealing with, and I can barely see in this rain!"

Ellie paused at the bottom of the tower, leaning against one of the tower's spindly metal legs, trying to catch her breath. Lightning forked the night sky to the west. Everything Ellie knew about lightning and electricity told her not to climb a tall metal thing during a storm. Heck, she shouldn't even be standing this close to a tall metal thing. But if she didn't help Parker stop the flooding, who would? And no matter what, she reasoned, they were probably safer together. So she grabbed the first rung and hoisted herself up.

The climb was more treacherous than Ellie had anticipated. The rungs were slick with rain and the wind tugged at her body, threatening to make her lose her grip. By the time she reached the halfway point, her body wanted to quit, but it was a long way down, so she reasoned it made more sense to keep going. "Don't look down, don't look down," she repeated to herself. She didn't want to think how high above the ground she was when one slip of her hand or her soggy wet boots could send her plummeting toward it.

When she finally neared the top of the ladder, she saw that Parker had hauled open the top hatch, secured it to its moorings, and was standing safely inside the structure atop a metal deck. "C'mon!" she yelled, waving Ellie toward the entry.

Carefully, so as not to slip on the slick metal, Ellie scrambled from the top of the ladder over to the open hatch. Parker helped her climb down inside the tower onto a small, round platform.

The deck led to a long, spiral staircase that wound its way around a support beam spanning the whole height of the tower. Ellie had expected to feel better once she was inside, safely shielded from the rain. But instead, she felt worse. A feeling of unease flooded her body, and she shook her head, trying to chase it away.

Parker had positioned herself about a quarter of the way down the steps and closed her eyes, preparing to exert her powers.

Ellie made her way down the narrow stairs, clutching at

the railing. Parker was already working, summoning the flood-waters through the hatch and into the tower. Ellie watched as the waterline near the bottom of the chamber slowly began to rise.

Parker groaned with the strain of her efforts. Ellie could feel how exhausted she was. She wished she could help, but her powers didn't include the ability to move water. She felt as frustrated as she was tired. Why had she come all the way up here just to stand and watch when there were animals in need of saving? Then she remembered how Parker must have felt when Ellie herself had been in this position—saving the trainload of people with powers she barely knew how to use, summoning forces and using skills that Parker didn't have. That day, Parker had just grabbed her hand, and suddenly it had felt like Ellie's whole body had filled with fresh air and new strength. That was the answer. She scrambled down the last few steps and reached for Parker's hand.

The bracelet on her own wrist went hot, warming the skin underneath and making her whole arm tingle. The waterline began to rise faster and faster. Parker squeezed Ellie's hand but never opened her eyes. She kept working. Ellie watched as the water filled the tower—first halfway, then two-thirds, then finally, until it nearly reached their feet, almost three-quarters of the way full.

"Good job, Parker," she said, gently. "We're almost there."

She stepped upward and placed her other hand on Parker's elbow, guiding her sister back up the steps. The water followed right below them.

Just as Ellie was starting to feel optimistic about the direction of this mission, she heard a sickening metallic sound. Parker's eyes shot open.

"What was that?"

The water stopped rising.

"I don't know," Ellie said, looking around for the source of the noise. Everything looked exactly as it had before. For a moment, everything was still.

"Just a little bit more and then we should probably go back," Parker said.

"Let's head back up to the platform," Ellie urged. "You can finish up there."

She barely had the words out when they heard a creaking noise. Ellie turned behind her just in time to see the top section of the staircase—the part that connected to the metal deck—make a clean break. They watched in horror as it fell into the water beneath them, slowing sinking into the murky depths.

"No!" Ellie screamed.

"How did that happen?" Parker yelled, her eyes wide with terror.

"I don't know!" Ellie cried in frustration. "It just broke off and fell! How are we going to get out of here? That space is too big for us to jump!"

"There has to be some way," Parker said. "Something we can use to bridge the gap. Can you summon some vines, maybe? Or a tree we can climb?"

"There aren't any vines out here in the plains. And how am I going to pull a whole tree in here? Those cottonwood trees are like seventy-five feet tall!"

"Eventually everyone will notice we're missing and come check on us, right?" Parker asked. "Maybe we can scramble up a parachute or something."

The sound of echoing footsteps filled the chamber.

"See!" Parker said, brightly. "They've come to look for us already!"

"Hello?" Ellie called. "Mom? Sadie? Finn?"

"Is someone up there?" Parker asked.

More metal footsteps.

"Hey!" Ellie yelled as loud as she could with her tired lungs. "Who's there?"

Clang. Clang. Clang. The footsteps continued for another moment, then stopped. A shadow appeared in the moonlight. Ellie could just make out a tall silhouette in the opening above them.

"Parker? Ellie?"

It was a familiar voice.

"Who is that?" Parker whispered.

It took Ellie a moment to place it.

"Aiden!" she exclaimed. "Hey, Aiden! The stairs are broken! We're trapped and we need help!"

Aiden appeared on the deck. "Oh, trust me, I am well aware." He flashed his perfect smile. Ellie looked into his gray eyes, which looked paler than usual in the moonlight. A sickening feeling washed over her.

"What are you doing here?' Parker asked.

"You didn't think that whole stairs thing was a coincidence, did you?" Aiden asked, leaning over the railing of the deck and smirking.

"What are you talking about?" Parker asked, confused.

Aiden's smirk split into a devilish grin.

"What I am saying, Parker, is that none of this has been a coincidence." His voice came out in a chilling hiss. "Not a single thing that has happened to you this summer. And it's all because of *me*."

CHAPTER EIGHTEEN

Parker's ears filled with the sound of her own pounding heart. It was so loud that it nearly drowned out every other sound—the wind, the water, the driving rain.

"It's you," she said, staring up at Aiden's smug grin. "You're the anomaly."

"Ooh! Someone's done their research! Well, aren't you *smart*," Aiden jeered. "Smart and powerful! Nothing gets by those McFadden twins, right?" He laughed. "Well, now you know my little secret."

Parker tried to think fast. What could she say to get Aiden to help them? Was there some part of him she could appeal to? Something she could possibly offer in exchange for letting them go? But looking into his cold eyes, she worried it was no use.

"Do you have any idea how hard it's been to pretend I'm *less* powerful than all of you?" he prattled on. "You whiny, spoiled brats spend all your time showing off for one another, talking about who's the most talented, who's the strongest, who still has all their powers. Like anyone cares." He laughed. "And all the while, sitting there thinking, 'poor Aiden, he doesn't have a twin, he's so sad and useless,'" he spoke in a mocking tone. "I just sat there and listened to it even though I'm more powerful than any of you! I have more power than all of you combined!"

"What do you want, Aiden?" Parker asked, puzzled. "You want to take over the Sentry so everyone will see how powerful you are?"

"Take over?" Aiden bellowed, taking a tone that managed to chill Parker's entire being. "No, I want to *destroy* it. I want to reclaim my rightful legacy from the families that stole it. The world has seen enough of the likes of the Powers and the Moreaus. It's time for a new order."

Ellie inhaled sharply. "But why would you want to destroy the Sentry?" she asked.

"You new recruits are all the same," Aiden rolled his eyes. "So small. So naive. So brainwashed by the idea of summer camp and *compasses* and *uniforms* and *missions*." He waved his arms and spoke in a squeaky voice as he added, "Look at me! It's just like being a spy! Oh no! Where's my compass?"

Parker's skin erupted into gooseflesh. Had Aiden been reading her thoughts?

"Yes, Parker," he said, by way of a reply. "I can and I have. I have all the powers of twins and then some. I can hear you, I can track you, I can follow you. No one and *nothing* is a match for me."

"I get it, you're powerful," Parker said. "But why hide that? Why not just be powerful together?"

"Because I don't agree with your worldviews. You're all so blinded by the excitement of having powers that you don't even stop to consider what it is you're doing."

"We're helping," said Ellie, hesitantly.

"We're saving the planet," Parker added. "By fighting the Danger."

"Wrong!" Aiden said, like a game show host pressing a buzzer. "You're making everything worse. The world *needs* the Danger. The Danger is part of the natural order."

Parker felt like her head was spinning. It was all she could do to grip the railing and try to hold herself upright.

"The Danger is what the world deserves. People have been wreaking chaos and destruction on this planet for decades. For centuries! The Danger is the natural response to *their* chaos and destruction. It's what they have coming to them! But the Sentry just keeps saving people from it. How does that make sense?"

Parker opened her mouth to argue but realized that she didn't know what to say. In a way, he was right. But was it better to let people, not to mention innocent animals, suffer?

"Oh, and the Sentry doesn't save *everyone*," Aiden continued, pacing. The metal deck groaned and clanged with every agitated step. "No, no. Not everyone. Just whomever they *choose*. Like they think they're some kind of *gods*." He spit the last word in disgust. "How do you choose who lives and dies?" he questioned, stopping his back-and-forth to cock his head at them. "Hmm? How?"

"I wouldn't choose," Parker said. "I would just try to help everyone I possibly could."

"And what, you would just let everyone die?" Ellie asked, her tone gaining an angry confidence that Parker wasn't used to hearing.

"Yes!" Aiden responded. "That's the only way they'll learn!"

"You can't learn if you're dead. So I'm sorry," Ellie said, shaking her head. "But I can't do that."

"Well, you won't have to do anything." Aiden sneered. "Because you're next."

"This isn't really about the Sentry," Parker said. "It's more personal than that."

Aiden's face suddenly hardened. It seemed that Parker had hit a nerve.

"You don't have a problem with the Sentry itself. You said you had a problem with the Moreaus and the Powers," she continued.

"Ginny Powers chose not to save my family," he growled. "A choice I've been trying to correct for years. No, Director Powers was too busy saving animals to care about my brother. Little did she know her carelessness would give me the power to bring her own family to an end!"

So that's what this was about. Parker remembered what Finn had said on her first day, about Aiden's brother dying in a tragic accident. She had no idea what had happened, but she knew her mother would have done anything in her power to save a child.

"I'm sorry for what happened to your brother," Parker said.

"No, you're not!" he spat back. "You're just saying that because you want me to let you go. But it's finally time for me to finish what I started. I'll admit when I was younger, my skills weren't quite so refined. But in a way, it's made it all the more fun! Enacting years of torture before I finally do you all in."

"What are you saying?" Ellie asked. "It's *you* who's been after our mom all this time?"

"Oh for goodness' sake, McFadden, do I have to spell it out for you?" Aiden threw his head back in exasperation. "I. Am. The. Danger. I have the power to summon it. To create it. To control it."

"But the Danger has existed for centuries," Parker countered.

"Ugh, not all the Danger," Aiden rolled his eyes. "But certainly every Danger *you've* ever come in contact with."

Parker remembered the Danger in the forest outside of Haven, how it had filled her head with those words, that *pain*. She flashed back to the Danger in the Greenhouse upon their arrival, and at the Tower just the night before. She thought of the Danger she'd encountered only hours ago, the way it had lashed out at her mother. All this time, she had thought the Danger was some otherworldly being, capable of using her worst fears, her deepest insecurities, against them. But all along, it had been Aiden.

Still, no matter who he was, no matter how much power he had, Aiden was still a human. And if Parker had learned anything in the last few days, it was that everyone—even people with powers—made mistakes. Everyone had fears. Everyone had regrets. And at the end of the day, everyone just wanted to be seen by someone, and for that someone to feel proud of them.

"Who's your mother, Aiden?" Parker asked.

"What?" Aiden snapped.

"Is that why you're doing all of this?" she interrogated.

"You don't know what you're talking about," he snarled.

"Because until a week ago, I thought my mother left me too," Parker pressed, "and it made me angry. All the time. And scared that it was my fault—"

"*Shut up!*" he roared. His voice echoed through the interior of the water tower. "Shut up shut up shut up! You think you know me, Parker? You think you're like me?" he sneered, his black hair falling into his face as he leaned out over the railing.

"No," she answered, "but I thought there was a lot to like about you. And I did think we were friends."

Aiden pulled back and tilted his head. He opened his mouth to say something, then closed it again, shocked into speechlessness.

"Enough of this!" he finally barked. "You think you can get me to abandon the plan I've been working on for seven years with a few emotional ploys? I've been working toward this long before you knew anything about the Sentry. And now I've reached the final step. This is the end of the Powers line, and this is the end of Mountain Harbor."

"Aiden," Parker said, taking the calm and steady tone of a hostage negotiator. "I'm sure the Sentry would welcome your thoughts about all of this—about the Danger and putting less effort into missions and more energy elsewhere. For what it's worth, you make a lot of excellent points, and I'm sure if you just gave them a chance, everyone would be willing to work with you." She hoped beyond all hope that she sounded convincing.

Aiden stared at her for one excruciatingly long moment.

"No," he said, simply, turning back toward the escape hatch. "This is where the story ends."

Before Parker could try to form another argument, the hatch door slammed shut. The tower was bathed in darkness. And, though she couldn't see it, Parker could feel the water level begin to rise again. But this time, it wasn't her doing.

"He's filling the tower," Ellie said, her voice laced with terror.

Within moments, the water had risen so high that the girls had to scramble to the topmost step to stay above the surface. As the water inched higher and higher, they began to kick their legs, treading water to stay afloat.

"I don't know how much longer I can do this," Parker said. "The tower is almost full."

Just when she was about to give up hope, the hatch popped open and the interior flooded with moonlight. Parker looked up, half afraid to see Aiden lording above them, but instead she was greeted by a familiar silhouette, complete with spiky hair.

"Thankfully, I used to be a lifeguard!" Finn said, shimmying out onto the deck and expertly extracting them from the water.

"I lost my boot!" Ellie yelled, over the wind. "My shoelace got stuck on the ladder and I had to let it go!"

"I've got extra gear in the chopper!" Finn shouted. As they climbed back through the hatch, Parker noticed the rain had stopped, but the wind had gotten louder—which meant it had gotten stronger. "But first, let's get out of here before the tornado gets any closer! Otherwise we'll be grounded here."

"Did you just say *tornado*?" Parker cried as she grabbed Finn's hand and scrambled out into the ladder.

"Yep," Finn groaned. "Our dear friend Aiden is really pulling out all the stops tonight. But too bad he forgot about one thing."

"What's that?" Parker asked.

"Me," Finn replied with a confident smirk. "And also science."

"Did you suspect him all along?" Ellie asked.

"Not until I saw him slinking around the plains," Finn said.

"Are my mom and Sadie okay?" Parker called.

"Yes," Finn said. "They're in the barn, with the animals. I'd just left them there as Aiden was making his getaway. Now where do we think he's headed next?"

"He's going back to Mountain Harbor," Parker said, without hesitation. "To destroy it."

"He controls the Danger," Ellie added.

"Yeah," Finn said. "I figured that might be the case when I watched him kinda *fly* out of here on a particularly feisty Fountainhead. We may not control the Danger, but I'm pretty good at flying! Let's all try to get back to the Harbor before it's too late."

Once they were safely down the water tower, the girls followed Finn through the muddy pasture at breakneck speed. Parker noted that, Aiden debacle aside, their plan for the mission had worked pretty well—only a few patchy puddles remained in the field, and the deeper flooding was gone. *Too bad it was all just a trap to get us all here*, she thought. One they had played right into.

They sprinted toward the barn, which creaked and groaned in the wind. The closer they got, the more it looked like it could disintegrate into scrap wood at any second. Parker picked up the pace, running ahead of the others, stretching her legs to their full span with every stride. She darted inside the big wooden entryway, scanning the room, running from stall to stall.

"Mom?" she yelled. "Sadie? Is anybody here?"

She saw lots of cattle, all safely tucked into their respective slots. But her mother and Sadie were nowhere to be found.

Parker ran back outside, where Finn and Ellie were just arriving.

"No one's there!" she yelled over the wind.

Then she heard it—that dreaded, familiar metallic screech ringing out in the air above her. Everyone looked up. She could just make out the smudgy wisps and inky tendrils of the Danger, emerging from a looming cloud.

"The Danger! It's still here!" Parker shouted.

"We have to keep moving!" Finn said, making a break back toward the helicopter. Parker and Ellie took off close behind.

"But what about Mom and Sadie?" Ellie called.

"We don't have time to fight this off with powers," Finn said.

"So what do we do?" Ellie uttered through panting breaths.

"Trust me," Finn said. "Get back near the helicopter. I have a plan."

True to their word, as soon as they'd all crossed the field, Finn slid their pack off their back, dropped it to the mud, and pulled out what looked like a cross between a large pen and a small flashlight. They aimed the thin black cylinder toward the Danger, sort of like a wizard or a sorcerer from a fantasy movie, and pressed a silver button with their thumb.

A beam of radiant white light shot out of the little wand. Parker followed the beam with her eyes and watched in awe as it met with the Danger. Immediately upon contact, the smoggy cloud disintegrated, taking its nauseating tendrils along with it. The whole thing happened so quickly that the Danger didn't even have time to shriek or howl in agony. Just *poof*! Gone. Without a trace.

"What—" Parker started to ask.

"Quartz laser," Finn said matter-of-factly, shoving the laser pen into their front pocket. They grinned. "Sometimes you don't even need powers when you have *science*."

"Have you been holding out on us?' Parker asked. She was astonished. How long had Finn had that tool? And why didn't they use it back at Mountain Harbor when the Danger attacked?

Ellie, as usual, refused to be distracted. "The Danger was hovering right over here," she said, pointing to a spot a few feet in the distance. "Given what we know about Aiden's motivations, I'd say that means Mom must be somewhere nearby."

"Mom?" Parker shouted, her hands cupped over her mouth to amplify the sound. "Sadie?"

"Mom?" Ellie shouted.

"We're over here!" came a tiny reply. The voice seemed to be coming from right next to them, and yet it sounded far away.

"Mom?" Parker called again, trying to follow the sound of her mother's voice.

"Down here!"

"It's a well," Finn shouted, pointing and rushing to a spot near to their feet. Sure enough, there was a deep hole in the ground, right under where the Danger had vanished.

Parker, Ellie, and Finn carefully circled the old stone well. The mouth of the well was lined with stones that stood maybe a foot high. Parker knelt onto the ground to get a better look. She couldn't make out any details in the darkness but could just about see two shadowy blobs waving up at her from the bottom.

"Thank goodness we already took care of the flooding," Ellie remarked.

"We've got to lower something down," Finn said. "There's rope back at the chopper."

"No, I think I've got this," Parker said, running her fingers along the stones. She thought about the stairs running along the side of the water tower. She thought about the granite bombs and learning to move stones. She pictured sliding some of these stones ever so slightly out of their spots in the well wall—not so much as to disturb the structure, but just enough that it would enable her mom and aunt to use them to climb out.

"We're going to make you some steps!" Parker called down into the well, her voice ricocheting back and forth between the sides of the circular wall and coming back to greet her as an echo. "Get ready to climb out!"

"Got it!" came their mom's voice.

"Are you sure these stones are big enough?" Sadie called back. "I have really big feet!"

"Leave it to you to make jokes at a time like this!" Ginny laughed.

"Well," Finn shrugged, looking at the twins in relief, "not only are they alive, but they're also in good spirits."

Parker and Ellie went to work, Parker placing all her focus on sliding stone by stone, and Ellie supporting her just as she had in the water tower. She moved up, row by row, searching for the right one, then wiggling it free of its mortar and sliding it just enough to be stepped on without coming free. As they pulled and slid, a ladder formed, and Ginny and Sadie's faces became clearer and clearer as they neared the mouth of the well. Parker worked ahead, sliding the stones above them to use as handholds to help keep their balance as their feet navigated the narrow steps. When they reached the top, Finn helped pull them both out and over the ledge.

"Thank you, Finn," Ginny gasped, wiping mossy green muck from her knees and jacket. "Who the heck was that horrible guy?"

"Aiden Baxter," the rest of them answered in unison.

"We can discuss his issues in the chopper," Finn said, "because I'm afraid we need to move. We think he's headed to Mountain Harbor right now to destroy it and everyone in it."

"I don't think I can fly us there in this wind," Sadie said. "Can you?"

"If we can get off the ground in the next five minutes," Finn replied, "then yes."

"Well, then, I guess we'd better run," Ginny said.

CHAPTER NINETEEN

The moment the helicopter landed at Mountain Harbor, Parker and Ellie jumped out of the tiny door, rushing inside as fast as their legs could carry them. Ellie was terrified of what she might find inside, but her need to find Aiden fully outweighed her fear.

The corridor was bathed in darkness as black smog filled the air, clouding their line of vision. Ellie held her hands out in front of her, desperately trying to clear a path. She heard boots behind her, running in all directions, their heavy footsteps echoing throughout the cavernous hall.

Finn whizzed by, bounding ahead of them, like a gazelle with a turbo powered motor. They held the quartz laser pen dagger-style in front of their body, ready to respond to the first signs of an attack.

They didn't need to wait very long.

A roar sounded from farther down the hall as the tentacles slithered out from all directions, inching closer to Ellie and Parker. With a dazzling flash of white light, Finn let loose another laser beam, disintegrating the Danger almost instantly. The tentacles shriveled and turned to dust. Ellie shuddered as she watched the smoky ash fall silently to the cavern floor.

"*Where* did you get that thing?" Parker asked, staring at the piles of ash.

"From me," said a voice, behind them.

Ellie turned to see none other than Barbara Boudin. She wore full-blown adventure gear—just like Finn's. Parker found it hard to believe this woman had ever been a librarian. Her glasses were gone, her hair was up in a braided bun tied with a bright red bandana, her khaki shorts were ripped at the mid-thigh, and her boots came up to her shin. She looked ready to raid an ancient tomb for treasure. Or to go fight the Danger.

"Remember, there's only enough battery in that for six more charges!" she called.

"I know!" Finn called back as they kept on running.

"I got in earlier," Boudin supplied, by way of explanation. "Michelle called after Sadie disappeared, and I knew where I needed to be."

"Is that the only laser?" Parker asked.

"Yes," she answered. "For now. Though clearly I need to make more."

A giant crash rang out from a far-off spot as the entire mountain trembled. Ellie half expected the whole place to come tumbling down around her. She heard shouts in the distance, followed by a sound that made her blood go cold—a dog's frantic barking.

"Arlo!" she yelled, taking off in the direction of the sound.

Glass shattered in the distance, followed by the unmistakable rainfall of shards hitting stone.

"The Greenhouse!" Parker cried.

They turned the corner and rushed down the hall to the Greenhouse, careening into someone's back as they reached the entrance. It was Jules, and she was retreating. Len stood in front of her, using her hands to try and push the smoke away, but even her best wasn't cutting it.

"We can't keep it back," Jules said. "I don't know what else to do."

Arlo crouched on the ground next to her, snarling and biting at the Danger but unable to do any damage as his teeth just gnashed through the smoke.

Oh, it's you! he thought, upon seeing Ellie. *I was worried! Glad you're back. Too bad about the snaky things, though. Things have been pretty bad around here. Annnnnd now you're pretty much caught up.*

"Where's everyone else?" Ellie asked.

"All over," Jules answered. "The Atrium, the Tower, the bunk wing—these things are everywhere!"

"You mean Aiden is everywhere," Parker grumbled.

"I can't hold it off any longer! We need to get everyone to the same place!" Len shouted over her shoulder.

"Then what?" Ellie questioned.

"Then we activate the fail-safe," Jules said. "But first, let's move!" She turned toward the hall, motioning for everyone to join her.

Len backed out through the Greenhouse doors, and Ellie and Parker slammed them shut behind her. They could hear the Danger slamming into the door, sounding like the weight of an angry rhinoceros. Ellie knew it was only a matter of time before it busted through to the other side.

The three of them rushed after Jules, accompanied by Arlo at Ellie's heels.

Let's go let's go let's go! he called, biting at the tendrils as they went.

"What's the fail-safe?" Parker asked.

"We all evacuate and this place self-destructs," Jules explained. "It exists in case of an absolute emergency. Explosives will detonate and bring the walls down."

"Won't the Danger just follow us?" Ellie asked.

"No. The energy the Sentry has imbued in all the stones and building materials should, hypothetically, be enough to trap the Danger in here," Jules explained.

"We can't destroy Mountain Harbor!" Parker argued, her voice panicked.

"If we don't, the Danger will," Jules stated plainly. "And take us down with it."

They followed Jules all the way up to the Atrium, and Ellie momentarily froze at the sight of the sheer chaos that greeted her. Broken furniture and shredded fabric littered the floor. Game pieces were strewn like confetti across the room. Lightning flashed here and ice bolts whizzed there. Terrifying black tentacles thrashed everywhere.

She spotted her mother and Sadie, ducked behind an upturned end table, clutching hands. She sprinted to them, Parker at her side. The twins crouched down next to them.

"Arlo, stay here where you're safe," Ellie said. He nodded and sat down next to her, ears alert.

Sadie's eyes were closed tight, her face and muscles straining.

"What should we do?" Parker asked.

"Granite bombs," Ginny said with a serious nod.

Parker's head whipped around the room, then back to Ginny.

"There aren't that many in here—if I pull out too many, I'll bring down half the cavern!" Parker protested, her pitch going higher and higher with every word.

"Parker," Ginny said, bringing her free hand to touch Parker's cheek, "if it's not you, it's either the Danger or the fail-safe. This place is going down one way or another."

Parker stalled, seemingly unable to summon her powers for what felt, to her, like an act of destruction.

"Honey, I promise that what I'm telling you to do is our best chance of survival," Ginny spoke calmly, and with complete confidence. "It's for all of us."

Ellie realized that though she never could have imagined these circumstances, in a roundabout way, she and Parker were getting what they'd always wanted. In their hardest moment, in their time of need, they were hearing their mom's advice.

She squeezed Parker's hand, hoping she would take it to heart.

"Don't worry. Just act," Ginny said. "And know that on the other side of this, no matter what, we will all be together."

"Okay," Parker said, nodding. Her lip trembled a bit as she let go of Ellie's hand.

Parker crawled to the fireplace, nearly on her stomach to avoid the blasts of wind Sadie was launching through the room from behind the table. Ellie watched as her sister started running her hands over the stones in the fireplace, just like she'd felt the walls of the cave, looking for pockets of energy.

"What should I do, Mom?" Ellie asked, never taking her eyes off Parker. She wanted to make herself useful. Something told her what she *needed* to do was make sure Parker stayed out of harm's way. Though, in the turmoil that surrounded them, that task seemed easier said than done.

In Ellie's peripheral vision, she saw icicles shooting through the air like crystalline darts, bits of twig and paper flying every which way, smudgy black wisps lashing to and fro.

Before her mother could answer, Boudin shouted from behind them. "Ellie! Come quickly!"

She glanced at her mother for approval as Ginny nodded. "Go."

Ellie scrambled to her feet and crouched next to Boudin, who was behind one of the room's stone pillars, using it as a shield. Ellie peeked out from behind the stone to watch Parker at work. Just as she had before, her sister loosened a giant slab from the Atrium wall and dragged it across the room in the direction of the Danger. The slab began to levitate, shaking with the energy inherent within it, until it finally launched in the direction of the Danger. Sparks flew through the air as the granite hurdled into the Danger's core, landing squarely in the center of its beating heart. Ellie shielded her eyes as the room erupted in a giant flash. When she opened them, she expected the Danger to be gone, crumpled into a pile of ash.

But this time, the granite bomb didn't destroy the Danger. It didn't even appear to lessen it. Instead, it made it *angry*.

"I—I don't know what happened," Parker stammered. "I think I chose the wrong stone."

The creature bellowed and roared with the force of a hundred car engines igniting at the same time. Its tentacles thrashed, slamming into walls, smashing everything they came in contact with. One tentacle swiped at the stone pillar in front of Ellie and Boudin, and they dove out from behind it just in time to avoid being crushed. Ellie skidded backward as the tenacle wriggled only yards away, jerking one way and then the other, as if trying to choose which direction to swipe—which direction to unleash its destruction.

"Ellie!" Gabby's voice came hurtling toward her through the dust and chaos. "Duck!"

Ellie did as she was told, dropping to the floor and flattening herself as much as possible. She felt something sail over her body as she covered the back of her head with her hands, the way she had learned to do during earthquake drills.

"It's time to amplify and activate!" Boudin's voice rang out above the din. "Everyone find their twin!"

Ellie made her way across the room and found Parker's hand.

"What's happening?" Parker whispered.

"This is the first step of the fail-safe plan," Ginny explained. "We make one final push with our twin powers, because we're stronger together. And if that doesn't work, we activate the fail-safe code."

"Well, actually this time there's one extra step," Boudin said. "Before we get to the fail-safe, we're going to sound the fire alarm. Because I loaded the sprinkler system with something special."

"Plant toxin?" Ellie asked.

"*Spurge*," supplied Parker, in that tone everyone used whenever they said it.

"Yes," Boudin nodded. "You've got that right. Ellie, Finn told me about what you did to direct the stream of toxin on the field in South Dakota. Do you think you can do that again?"

"I can try," Ellie nodded.

"I can help," Parker said.

"Great." Boudin smiled. "Once we're all here, joined together, it will lure the Danger to our center. As soon as the sprinklers are activated, I need you to direct as much of the toxin as you can—create a stream and try to surround it. Once it starts to weaken, aim it directly into its center."

Ellie gave a nod that no doubt looked more confident than she felt. She remembered what Finn had told them about the milky spurge—how it didn't actually defeat the Danger but only weakened it. She worried that no matter how much of it she was able to send in the Danger's direction, it wouldn't be enough. But she was willing to do her best. What other choice did they have?

She looked around the room at all the twins who were now gathered and holding hands—Jules and Len, Gray and Gabby, Cassie and Casey, Sadie and Mom. Finn stood alone, gripping the laser pen in one hand and petting Arlo in the other, which Ellie figured was the next best thing.

That left just one person.

Moreau rushed into the room, joining her sister, Barbara Boudin.

"Do you have the code?" Barb asked, and Moreau nodded yes.

As if on cue, a terrible laugh—the same laugh Ellie had once thought of as contagious—filled the room.

"Awww! How cute is this?" Aiden said, his voice echoing from nowhere and everywhere at once. The Danger responded to the sound of his voice, swaying and dancing with every word. "It looks like someone has watched too many wholesome cartoons. *Twin power!*" he taunted. "You think if you all hold hands, you can beat me? Like your cute little powers will multiply. That's so sweet! And so hilariously misguided."

Where was his voice coming from? Ellie scanned the room, squinting through the dense fog. She spotted him, dressed in all black, lurking behind the largest swaying Danger cloud.

"Did you all forget that I've trained with you? I've lived next to you for years! I know your secrets. I know how all your little plans work. You can't possibly defeat me. Give up!" he shouted, his voice chilling Ellie to the bone.

"We won't give up," Moreau said.

"Give me Ginny Powers and control of the base and no one gets hurt," Aiden snapped. "I will let you leave the premises without touching any of you. You have my word."

The twins held strong, clasping hands, none of them moving a muscle. Even Arlo didn't so much as blink.

"All right! Have it your way," Aiden said, as the murky clouds started to whine and hum around them. "But don't act like I didn't try to negotiate."

Ellie squeezed Parker's hand. As the monstrous creatures started to roar, she leaned over to her sister. "No matter what happens, Parker, I'm going to do my best," she whispered. "I promise, I will protect you."

Parker turned to look at Ellie, her eyes wide.

"What did you say?"

"I will protect you," Ellie repeated.

I will protect you.

"That's it!" Parker said. "I have an idea."

CHAPTER TWENTY

I will protect you.

The words played over and over again in Parker's head.

The words that had come from the little red gem in the hallway. Sadie's imprint.

"What is it?" Ellie asked.

"I don't know," Parker said, "maybe it's nothing, but it could be something. You focus on the plant milk. I'll take care of the rest."

Parker scanned the room. She desperately wanted to talk to her mom and Sadie. But Aiden's gray eyes were trained right on them. If she so much as dared to move a muscle, he'd unleash the Danger on them. Or worse.

Mom can hear our thoughts, right? Parker thought at Ellie.

"Hypothetically, yes," Ellie whispered back. "But in that case, so can Aiden."

She had a point.

Unless Aiden doesn't understand what we're talking about. I'm going to think really hard about something I want Mom to ask Sadie, okay? Parker thought. *Can you listen to see if she responds?*

Ellie nodded. Then Parker thought as hard as she could, so hard that she could feel the blood pulsing in her brain.

Sadie, what are the gems in the hallway? Do they all have strong imprints like yours?

Parker's heart fluttered with hope as she watched Ginny lean forward and whisper something to Sadie.

Ellie squeezed her hand, then quietly said, "Sadie says the answers are *spinel* and *yes*."

"Surrender!" Aiden taunted, his voice echoing in the eerie quiet of the large chamber. "This is it, Sentry! You know you can't win. This is your last chance to admit defeat before I turn this place into a pile of rubble."

I have to get to the mosaic hallway, Parker thought at Ellie.

"Parker—there's a Danger blocking that hallway!" Ellie protested under her breath. "I'm supposed to wait for Ms. Boudin to trigger the sprinklers—and I need your support when it happens! What is this about?!"

Don't worry, I only need a minute. I'll be back in time for the spurge. *I just need one more thing to finish them off once you weaken them. And if I'm right, those gems in the mosaic are just the thing.*

"Okay," Ellie whispered. "I trust you. How do we do this?"

We have to wait until he's distracted. As soon as the sprinklers start, I'll be back before you know it.

Ellie just sighed.

"We'll never surrender, Aiden," Moreau said. "And all the threats in the world will never change that."

"Fine!" Aiden bellowed. "Suit yourself."

The Danger began to roar, its angry sounds barely covering up Aiden's laughter. As the room erupted in chaos, Parker and Ellie released their grip on each other's hands as Parker ran, full sprint, toward the mosaic hallway. Behind her, Parker could hear a cacophony of smashing and thrashing and thumping, but she kept her eyes straight ahead, moving as fast as she could to her secret weapons.

A fine mist scattered through the air as the sprinklers were deployed. Parker rounded the final turn and shot into the mosaic hallway, hoping that Ellie was all right without her.

Just another minute, Parker thought with all her might. *Just another minute and I've got you.*

But for now, she needed to focus.

"All right, spinel," she said, out loud. "Who wants to help me?" She focused on the stones, locking into their energy until she could hear the imprints of the most courageous, committed, and powerful of the bunch.

I will always fight for the future of the planet, said one stone as Parker wiggled it loose from the mosaic and collected it in her grasp.

We are stronger together, said the next stone.

Good must prevail, said the third.

Parker continued down the hall, working quickly to unearth a gem for each current member of the Sentry. She stopped before the last spinel, allowing the message of its imprint to wash over her.

I see you. I love you. I'm proud of you. It's time to do what's right.

She would recognize that voice anywhere. It was her mother's.

Without wasting an instant, Parker took off in a run. She tore through the halls, back toward the Atrium, where she was greeted with an epic roar.

Amid shouting and crashing, Parker watched as a wide ribbon of the milky toxin danced through the air, winding itself through the room to coil around the Danger. One massive inky cloud hovered in the center of the room, swirling like a cyclone, its tendrils thrashing wildly outward in all directions.

The sets of twins all stood pressed against the walls for fear of coming within the tendrils' reach.

"It's no use!" Aiden's voice boomed above the din. "I can outlast you all!"

There was so much chaos that Parker was able to slip into the room unnoticed. She lurked along the walls, handing her special glistening parcels to each person as she passed.

"Spinel bomb," she whispered to Gray, whose eyes lit up with recognition.

"Good thinking!" he said. Even under the circumstances, it made Parker blush.

"Hold this and wait until I give you the signal," she whispered, over and over, as she made her way along the perimeter. "Then let it fly and let me do the rest."

"Incredible," said her mother.

"That's genius!" Sadie said, grinning at the red stone.

"No, you and Ms. Boudin are the geniuses," Parker smiled. "It's your research. I'm just following your lead. It's like you told me at the entrance. Lots of small stones make one very powerful wall."

And with that, Parker slipped in place behind Ellie, allowing all her remaining strength to funnel to her twin. Her bracelet glowed hot against her wrist as the stream of toxin grew stronger, winding faster and faster around the massive Danger. All the remaining smoke in the room flew to the center creature, trying to sustain it, but it continued to cower and shrink.

A heart-stopping wail rang through the air, and at first

Parker wasn't sure whether it had come from Aiden or the Danger. But now she saw—it was both.

As the smoke swirled faster and faster into a column, Parker could just make out the shape of a person hovering where its beating heart would normally be. Aiden had stepped into its vortex, sacrificing himself to become one with the Danger, funneling all his energy into one last effort to retain its power.

"This is your last chance, Aiden," Moreau spoke, stepping forward. "We would never forsake you. If you make this stop, we'd be willing to talk. We could do things differently in the future. We can listen to what you have to say."

"NO!" he shouted, as the inky cyclone began to glow. Parker couldn't help but notice it was the same glistening translucent shade of gray as Aiden's eyes. "How dare you try save me like you're some kind of hero. I don't need saving. And I don't need you! As soon as your little milk runs out, you'll have no choice but to activate the fail-safe. So let me put you out of your misery. Say goodbye to Mountain Harbor!"

"Not so fast!" Parker yelled, holding her gem in the air. She handed the remaining one to Ellie, who did the same.

All around the chamber, every recruit held their gem up in the air.

"Ready, aim, fire!" yelled Parker.

The gems went hurling through the air. Some with wind, some with fire, some with lightning. Some with ice or water or roots. Parker held her palms up to the Danger, straining to move the gems into the core of the massive cloud, to whatever remained of Aiden's heart.

The force of the imprints was so powerful that if they hadn't already been standing near the chamber's walls, it would have surely pushed them back against it. Parker winced against the loudest sound she had ever heard as the Danger disappeared in a series of flashes, like a strobe light flashing white and then gray and then scarlet.

And then, it was over. The room was bathed in silence.

The Danger was gone. And so was Aiden.

CHAPTER TWENTY-ONE

Parker moved quickly across the mess hall, skirting around each table to place one sunshine yellow napkin at every setting. Ellie followed close behind, outfitting each napkin with silverware.

"Teamwork makes the dream work," Jules joked, carrying a massive platter of sugar cookies in from the pantry. She placed it in the center of the bounty that was already spread across the buffet table.

"Unless your name is Aiden," Len remarked, looking troubled. Then she added a massive pitcher of lemonade to round off the display. "That looks nice!" she said, her expression brightening. She stepped back to admire their handiwork.

There was a fruit salad made with the leftover harvest from when they last fixed the Greenhouse. (Something that was starting to feel like a daily occurrence.) There were sandwiches and pasta and an extremely fancy-looking cheese plate. There was a cake, adorned with white icing and colorful hand-frosted flowers, courtesy of Jules. And of course, there were the cookies, which the girls had just baked that morning, in honor of multiple occasions.

A banner hung behind the table read, "WELCOME BACK, GINNY AND BARB!" in haphazard rainbow lettering. But everyone knew they had even more to celebrate. Against all odds, Mountain Harbor was still standing, and so were its recruits. Casey and Cassie and Gray and Gabby had left the base early that morning, heading back to their homes for the rest of the summer. Thankfully, they were all unharmed, but after Aiden's final bid for power left them all a bit shaken, Moreau said anyone who felt safer off-base was welcome to call their parents, and they had taken her up on the offer.

That left the four of them—Ellie, Parker, Jules, and Len—to hang back with their Sentry-bound parents. Ellie was amazed at all they had accomplished, including putting this party together with virtually no planning and very little sleep. But she supposed that excitement was basically its own superpower.

Early that morning, Ellie, Parker, and their mom had video-chatted with their dad for a whole hour, catching him up as best as they could on how much mayhem they'd encountered in such a short time. "Are you serious?" he kept asking, his eyes growing wide, at every new detail they shared with him. Ellie had never seen any of them so happy, but the best was yet to come. By now, he was already on a flight headed their way so they could reunite in person.

This little party—a surprise for the adults—had been Finn's idea, but everyone immediately agreed. At their urging, they'd all met up in the mess hall, one of the few rooms not ravaged by the Danger, to get everything in place. And now, they waited for their guests to arrive for what they expected to be a normal lunch.

"What matters most," Finn said with a smile, "is that we're all together. And there's no better way to celebrate than with a big pile of cookies, don't you think?"

"Here they come!" whispered Jules, as everyone ran into place beneath the sign.

Ellie heard the rumble of footsteps in the corridor, along with the murmur of voices. It was such a nice change to hear these regular everyday sounds, after a day filled with running and stomping and shouting. The four adults entered the mess hall, each paired off with the other's twin: Ginny talking earnestly to Moreau, with Sadie and Barb giggling behind them.

"SURPRISE!" Ellie and the others yelled in unison.

"What is this?" Ginny looked genuinely shocked.

"Oh my goodness!" Boudin clapped her hands in delight.

"Welcome back!" Finn yelled.

The adults made their way over to the buffet table, taking in the spread.

"This is so sweet," Ginny remarked, hugging Parker and then Ellie. "Thank you."

"No one gave me a party when I came back," Sadie muttered playfully.

"That's because Michelle doesn't like you," Ginny teased.

Moreau made a *tsk* sound with her tongue. "Now, now," she said. "That's all water under the bridge. I'm glad we're all here, together, and that everyone is safe."

"See?" Ginny laughed, elbowing Ellie. "What did I tell you? Everyone loves a reunion!"

For a few moments, they milled about, talking, laughing, and filling plates with food. Ellie looked around the room, feeling happier than she'd ever remembered feeling. And so, for that matter, did everyone else. Even Moreau was uncharacteristically light, talking in a happy, singsong voice that Ellie had never heard her use before.

"All right everyone," Moreau said, tapping a fork on the side of her glass to get their attention. "I have an announcement to make. As it turns out, this very lovely welcome party is something else as well." She paused for effect. "It's also a celebration of our new leadership—and my retirement."

The room fell silent for a moment. Ellie had thought this day was a happy occasion, but now she wasn't so sure.

"Now, this is honestly something I've been thinking about for a while. We all know recruitment has been down in recent years, and I think it might be good for the base to have some new blood to help liven things up around here."

Everyone looked around the room, making eyes at each other, unsure of how to react.

"After the events of this past week, I feel more ready than ever to move on. All of you wonderful young people have already inherited a planet that's filled with greater challenges than I've ever faced, and the least I could do is offer you my support as an effective leader. That includes knowing when it's time to pass the baton. I'm sorry for how much tragedy you've witnessed in such a short amount of time. But your actions made the difference. I want you to know that you've all impressed me very, very much."

"Now, Michelle," Boudin cut in. "You have more experience than anyone. There will always be traitors and troubles and surprises. You know as well I do, that's just part of the territory."

"Yes," Sadie said, nodding. "We all feel you've done an excellent job as director." She paused before adding, "Even me."

"Thank you," Moreau said. "But be that as it may, the Sentry needs protecting now more than ever, and I no longer have the drive the job requires. I'm ready to kick back on a hammock with a frozen smoothie in one hand and a romance novel in the other." Parker and Ellie shared an amused look. "To that end, Instructor DeSoto and I have discussed what leadership might look like in the future." She glanced over at Finn. "Instructor? Would you like to take it away?"

"Sure thing," Finn said, grinning from ear to ear as they stepped forward to take the stage. "Now, I know what you're all thinking. This must mean I'm going to be the next director. Well, I'm pleased to announce that you are very—wrong." Finn snort-laughed at their own joke. "There's a reason they call me Instructor DeSoto! Teaching is my passion—management, not so much. My job suits me perfectly, and I plan to do it for as long as I am able."

Ellie was glad to hear it. Not because she didn't think Finn would be an excellent leader—they had single-handedly saved her at least five times over the last two days. But Finn really was a phenomenal teacher and she wanted them to keep doing it. Especially if she and Parker were going to continue their training.

"Director Moreau, if I may still call you that, and I discussed how we might change the way things are done around here," Finn looked slowly around the room, their eyes stopping to meet everyone else's as they spoke. "And we decided that in a place with so many special abilities, it makes sense for people to really lean into those talents. So, I am pleased to appoint Barbara Boudin as the Director of Research and Development, effective immediately."

Ms. Boudin blushed as everyone broke into a smattering of applause.

"As such, you will have an ample budget for investigating

crystals, Fountainheads, and whatever your heart desires," Moreau said.

"And making more quartz laser pens!" Finn added.

"Congratulations!" everyone said, raising their glasses.

"Who will take over training?" Parker asked. "I mean, I know Instructor DeSoto will still be handling classes, but who will be in charge of the overall curriculum and offering advice on big topics?"

Finn held one finger in the air. "Excellent question! I'm glad you asked. We were thinking *that* job might best be served by two different individuals with very different styles and a wealth of experience between them. Any guesses as to who it is?"

"Well, I know it isn't me," Jules joked.

Ellie was surprised to hear it. She half expected Moreau to name Jules as the next director.

"It's not?" Parker said, not bothering to hide her surprise. Clearly, she'd been thinking the same thing.

Jules shook her head no. "I think the last few days have made me feel similar to how my mom does," she said, with a shrug. "And I've been thinking it might be nice to step away for a while. See how life is outside of this place. I mean, I've spent the last seven years here!" She paused before concluding. "I dunno, I've always dreamed of going to fashion school.

But that doesn't mean I won't come back. And when I do, I'm designing new uniforms." That prompted a laugh.

"What's wrong with a mock turtleneck?" Ginny asked.

"Everything is wrong with a mock turtleneck," Sadie replied, under her breath.

Finn continued with the announcement. "Well, since none of you had any guesses, I'm pleased to announce that Ginny and Sadie Powers will be named as Consulting Co-Chiefs of Legacy Matters, reporting to Barbara Boudin. Congratulations, both."

"Woo-hoo!" Parker cheered, at full volume, the way she did from the sidelines of her Ultimate games (though as a starting player, she was rarely on the sidelines).

"Yeah, Mom!" Ellie added. "Go, Aunt Sadie!"

"And that leaves just one position," Finn said, an air of mystery creeping into their voice.

Parker and Ellie exchanged a glance.

Who could it be? Ellie wondered. Pretty much everyone else in the room had already been given a new title. That is, everyone except for Len. Len was nineteen and had been here just as long as Jules. She had as much knowledge and experience, and equally as much talent. So it must be Len. But she had never really seemed like the leadership type.

"Well, not to ruin the surprise or anything," Len spoke. "But it isn't me. The Sentry's been amazing, and I definitely want to come back to teach someday. But if Jules is getting to experience life on the outside, I want to do it too. And there are an awful lot of sports and classes and concerts that have my name on them."

"That sounds wonderful," Finn said.

That meant there were just two possible candidates left. All eyes slowly turned to Parker and Ellie.

Well, this was awkward. Ellie stared down at her plate, hoping her half-eaten cookie might save her from her mounting embarrassment.

Would they pick just one of them? Which twin would it be?

Ellie prepared herself for the inevitable disappointment. She had done an awful lot over the last few days—with thorns and vines and toxic plant milk—and she was proud of what she'd accomplished. But in the end, Parker had been the real hero. She was the one with the flashier powers. Parker was the one who could hear imprints and create granite bombs. In the end, the spinels had been her idea. And that's what had saved them all.

"I am very pleased to announce..." Finn began. Ellie reached over and squeezed Parker's hand, ready to congratulate her. "Ellie and Parker McFadden, our youngest ever junior co-directors of Mountain Harbor Base."

What?

Parker was already jumping up and down. "We did it, Ellie!" she was saying. "This is amazing! We're like, King of the Spies!"

Ellie looked to their mother to confirm that it was real.

"I know this might seem like an unorthodox decision," Moreau cut in. "But I feel very certain that you two are up for the job. With all I've seen over your short time in these halls, I can say without hesitation that you are not only quite capable when it comes to your talents but also unmatched when it comes to your creativity, courage, and leadership."

Ellie couldn't believe her ears. Parker vibrated a little bit next to her, teeming with excitement.

"Now," Moreau pointed one finger at them, sliding back into the stern, intimidating persona they were used to seeing. "You are not to interpret this as a sign that you are done with your training, nor with your growth. That is why you have our senior leaders—your mom, Sadie, and Ms. Boudin—to help oversee your development. As well as certain administrative matters as you attend to your regular schoolwork. And of course, should you ever need me—for help or advice or anything at all—I am always just a phone call away."

"Thank you," Ellie nodded, feeling a small tear forming in her eye. She tried to keep it from spilling over, thinking it probably wasn't a good look for a junior director to start her tenure by immediately crying into her cookie. But when she looked over at her mother, then at Sadie, then at everyone else around them, she was shocked to discover there wasn't a dry eye in the house.

"I couldn't be happier," Ginny said, clasping her hands in front of her.

"Thanks, Mom," Parker said, wiping her own lone tear from her cheek.

"I can't wait to tell your father!" their mother laughed. "It looks like he may be working on assignment from here for a while."

"Ooh, he's going to *love* that," Sadie joked.

Ellie looked down as something furry brushed up against her leg.

Congratulations! Congratulations! Can I have a cookie? Congratulations! Arlo beamed up at her, furiously wagging his tail.

She reached down to give him a scratch under his chin. "Thank you!" she said. "And no, you cannot have a cookie. Did you seriously think that would work?"

I dunno, it was worth a try. He made a goofy face before slinking away, likely to go beg a cookie off of somebody else.

Ellie and Parker broke away from the others, slowly wandering off to a corner table where they'd have a better view of the room.

"Junior co-director," Ellie said, sighing contently. "Who would've thought?"

"Certainly not Mabel."

"It was a rhetorical question."

"But really," Parker said. "What do you think about all this?" She waved her hand in the air, indicating the massive, largely destroyed underground base that was now, improbably, their responsibility.

"I think we did good," Ellie nodded. "And I think we have a lot more to learn."

"That is so like you," Parker said. "Already finding some reason to worry."

"Who said I'm worried?" Ellie laughed.

For once, she didn't feel frightened at all. Sure, she might not have perfect control over her powers. She might not be able to predict what would happen in the future. She might not have any idea what was expected of them as soon as this party was over. But as far as Ellie was concerned, she knew all she needed to know. As long as they were together, they could tackle anything.

ACKNOWLEDGMENTS

We'd like to thank our partners, Chris and Trevor, who did what the best teammates do and encouraged us throughout this adventure. For the true "nature girl" in our family, Kristina, we are thankful every day for your enthusiasm, activism, knowledge, and pure love of our planet and its beauty. Thank you to Todd, Erica, and Dara for your belief in the Powers from the beginning and for helping us find its perfect home. Anne, thank you for your incredible support; you are magic. Thank you to Laura, whose energy and expertise made the writing process fun; and to Caroline, whose capable hands lent our story extra sparkle. Finally, thank you to Marty, the real-life Arlo—equally loyal and sassy—who took his job of supervising writing sessions very seriously (and was rewarded with many cookies).